"I had a wond[...] at-
urday night," said M[...]

"So did I," Stephen interrupted. "Holly and
the others thought you were a real find."

"And I liked them, too," she said sincerely.
"But things are...well...I don't know just
how to put this," she hesitated.

Stephen simply looked at her, waiting for her
to say what was on her mind.

"What I mean to say," she began again, "is
that even though I had a good time, I can't
come to your parties any more, and we can't
meet and...hold hands or anything. It just
isn't possible."

"What did I do?" Stephen asked, bewildered.

"Oh, it's not you, believe me—you're one
of the nicest boys I've ever met. It's me—
it's something that was going on long before you ever moved here. See, I'm Kip Morgan's girl," Missy finally said, "and that
means I stick by him—always. I belong to
him."

The
Preppy
Problem

BY

Stephanie Austin

FAWCETT JUNIPER ● NEW YORK

RLI: $\dfrac{\text{VL: 7 + up}}{\text{IL: 8 + up}}$

A Fawcett Juniper Book

Published by Ballantine Books

Library of Congress Catalog Card Number: 83-91213

ISBN 0-499-70036-4

Manufactured in the United States of America

First Ballantine Books Edition: March 1984

FOR ETHEL AND IRA

One

"MELISSA!" HER father called from the hallway, "tell Kip you'll call him back later. I told the McRaes we'd be there by 7:30 and it's almost that now."

Missy jumped down from the tall kitchen stool, trying to untangle herself from the long, white phone cord that had wound itself around her waist. "Oh Kip, I promised my parents I'd go with them to see these old friends of theirs who just moved here to Highland Park from Boston and..."

"Melissa!" Mr. Cartwright's voice boomed again.

"Oh boy, he's really getting all uptight—I gotta go. Listen, tell everybody 'hi' for me, and if we don't stay too late, I'll call you when I get home. Luv ya." Missy hurriedly hung up the phone and raced toward the closet to get her coat, her long blond hair flying behind her.

"All set, Missy?" Mrs. Cartwright asked as she watched her daughter readjust the collar of her madras plaid blouse, button up her navy blue cardigan, and then bundle into her navy pea coat.

Missy nodded as she pulled on her cornflower-blue crocheted angora beret that exactly matched the color of her huge, long-lashed eyes. She grabbed her navy shoulder bag from the hall table and slid her knee-socked feet into her Frye boots, tucking in the cuffs of her beige corduroy pants. "Okay, I'm set," she said as she wound her matching angora scarf around her neck and pulled on her mittens, "but I still don't know why I have to go with you. The McRaes don't even know me."

Mr. Cartwright opened the door and waited for his wife and daughter to join him on the front porch. "Well, they knew you as a baby, let's see...you were about six months old when we moved out here, and their son Stephen was about the same age. My goodness, Anne," he said to his wife, "that was over fifteen years ago. Both 'babies' are now sixteen." Mr. Cartwright smiled and patted his daughter's shoulder. "How come fifteen years has made you so pretty and has made me so old?" he asked her, laughing.

Missy smiled back at him, shivering in the fierce Chicago winter wind that propelled them down the block toward the old fieldstone house where Frank and Jeanne McRae had just moved in. "Oh Dad, you didn't look so old on the racquetball court last week when you beat Kip to pieces. He told me he hopes he's in such good shape when he's forty."

"Please, don't remind me," Mr. Cartwright said, grinning, as they fought against a drift of snow that the wind blew over them. "You know," he continued, "Frank McRae and I have been friends ever since we were Kip's age. When we were sixteen we planned on forming our own law firm, but then Frank went off into journalism and we moved to Chicago when I got a job with my firm. Life sort of took us in separate directions. When Frank called and told me he'd taken a job at the *Tribune* and wanted a house outside the city, I convinced him to buy the old Monroe house. Funny how things work out—after all these years, here we are, living down the block from one another in a suburb of Chicago, our kids going to the same high school."

"We're going to have to shovel the walk again by the time we get home," Mrs. Cartwright said as they turned up the path toward the McRaes' and rang the bell. "Look, Jeanne's already hung blue curtains in the window. That's just like Jeanne to find such a wonderful color. You'll like her, Missy—she's always a lot of fun," her mother whispered as they huddled together and waited for a McRae to answer the door.

"What would really have been fun would have been for me to have gone with Kip to watch *Superman II* on Buffy's dad's video cassette machine. Everybody else is going to be there—everybody except me," Missy grumbled as Mrs. McRae opened the door.

"Here you are," she said brightly. "Ooh, come on in—it's freezing out there. Frank! Stephen! The Cartwrights are here," she called over her shoulder as she showed them into the house. "Please excuse the moving mess—most of the boxes are unpacked, but there are still a few heaps of chaos scattered here and there. Oh, Annie, you look marvelous," Mrs. McRae said, hugging Missy's mother and then kissing Mr. Cartwright on the cheek. She then turned to face Missy. "And Melissa, what can I say? You're beautiful, just beautiful," she repeated, running her hand over Missy's honey-blond hair that fell in a straight, blunt-edged cascade to the middle of Missy's back. "Oh, Thom, Anne, you must be so proud of her."

"That we are," Mrs. Cartwright answered, smiling. "An honor student and queen of the junior winter carnival to boot."

"Who's queen of the carnival?" Frank McRae thundered as he came into the hallway and greeted his old friends warmly. Although Mr. Cartwright was almost six feet tall, his height was diminished by the massive form of Frank McRae, whose size was equaled only by his own good humor. "Wow," he exclaimed, looking over at Missy, "you two outdid yourselves with this one! I mean, Jim is a good-looking boy," he said, referring to Missy's older brother who was a freshman at Boston University and had visited the McRaes in the fall, "but she's a knockout! Where is that son of mine anyway?" he said, looking over his shoulder toward the stairs that led up to the bedrooms. "Stephen! Come on down here—our guests have arrived." Mr. McRae turned back toward the group assembled in the hall. "You'll have to excuse him—he's writing a short story and doesn't like to be disturbed while he's working. Why don't we go into the living room? I've lit a fire and Jeannie's made some hot cider. Thom, you didn't tell us how cold Chicago was going to be. That wind can blow you right into the lake!"

Missy followed her parents and the McRaes into the warm, firelit room, glancing at the grandfather clock in the corner as she sat down on the soft, blue-chintz sofa. Eight o'clock—*Superman II* would have already started. Oh, well, she thought to herself, at least it's on a cassette. Maybe Buffy would let her see it another time. She could just picture what was going on in the Sanders's den at this very moment. Mrs. Sanders and Buffy would have popped a huge bowl of popcorn, and the card table would be set up in the corner with cans of Cokes—and Diet Dr. Pepper for Buffy and Missy—bowls of cheese curls and Ruffles, and a huge plate of carrot sticks, celery, and cherry tomatoes to dip in the yogurt and onion soup mixture that Buffy concocted earlier that evening.

"Let the guys stuff themselves with junk if they want to," she had told Missy on the way home from school, "I'm sticking to the carrots." Unlike Missy, who could eat anything she wanted and still remain a size six, Buffy had always battled to remain a size eleven, and her favorite topic of conversation was always her weight. Missy smiled to herself, thinking of the whole crowd gathered around the television, some on the couch, some sitting on the floor. She could just see Kip Morgan's long, khaki-covered legs sprawled out on the Sanders's white shag carpet, the bowl of cheese curls already in his lap, the orange crumbs littering his cream-colored tennis pullover with the navy and maroon stripes around the collar and cuffs. His light brown hair would be falling softly over one corner of his forehead, and his gray eyes would stare intently as Superman flew out at him from the television screen. They would all be there, all the members of The Group, Missy thought: Kip, Tink Winslow, Poodie Hawkins, Win Winthrop, Tish Honeywell, Jimbo Ryan—everybody, except Missy.

"Would you like some cider?" a voice asked, intruding on Missy's happy little vision and bringing her back

to the McRaes' living room where a slim, broad-shoul-
dered boy with thick, dark-brown hair and piercing
green eyes was holding out a steaming mug before her.

"Mmm, thanks," Missy said, taking the mug and
inhaling the fragrant cloud of cinnamon and apples
that rose from the hot liquid.

"This is Stephen, at last," Mrs. McRae said, laughing, as she re-entered the living room carrying a plate
of crackers and cheese from the kitchen. "We've finally
succeeded in prying him away from the typewriter.
Whenever we can't locate him, Frank and I listen for
the sound of either the typewriter keys or a clarinet,
and then we just follow the sound."

"Mother," Stephen groaned, embarrassed by her
gentle teasing, his cheeks turning slightly pink.

"So you play the clarinet, huh, Steve?" Mr. Cartwright began.

"Yes, I do," Stephen answered. He hesitated slightly
before he spoke again. "Uhm, I like to be called Stephen, not Steve. I'm not very fond of nicknames. A little
too preppy for my tastes."

Now Missy's cheeks began to burn and she turned
toward Stephen who had sat down in the rocking chair
near the fireplace. "And what's wrong with being a
preppy?" she asked him sharply.

Mrs. McRae shot Stephen a warning look as he
opened his mouth to speak. "Nothing, nothing's wrong
with being a preppy. I guess some people like being
called Flopsey and Mopsey and..."

"Stephen," his father broke in, "Melissa's a junior
at Highland Park High, too. Maybe she could give you
a little idea of what to expect on your first day. When
do you head back anyway, Melissa? Monday?"

"No," she answered. "Second semester officially starts on Tuesday. Monday is an institute day and the teachers all have to be there, but we don't." She looked over at Stephen, who was watching her intently, and then turned back to Mr. McRae. "And please, Mr. McRae, call me Missy. I happen to like nicknames very much." Feeling her cheeks beginning to flush again, Missy lowered her eyes and took a long, slow sip of the cider.

The sound of a throat being cleared preceded Stephen's voice. "Um, Missy, do they have a good orchestra at Highland Park?"

Missy looked up at him and nodded her head. "I guess so—they give Christmas and Easter concerts every year, and they play for all of the musicals. Are you going to try out?"

Stephen's face brightened and a shy smile crossed his face, causing two dimples to appear in his cheeks. "Yes, definitely. I was first chair clarinetist at my old school in Boston. Do you play any instruments?"

Missy shook her head and took a piece of the cheese Mrs. McRae was offering her.

"Why don't you two go into the den where you won't have to shout above the rest of us," Mrs. McRae suggested. "You can take your cider in with you. Go ahead, you don't really want to stay here with us, do you?"

Stephen rose from his chair, and Missy followed him through the kitchen and into the wood-paneled den where Stephen sat down in an overstuffed armchair and Missy found a place on the couch. Neither of them spoke, and Missy looked out the huge picture window frosted around the edges with lacy icicles. The snow was still falling hard, and the room was chilly after the warmth of the living room fire.

Missy pulled her sweater more tightly around her. If Kip were here, she thought, he'd offer me his sweater. She looked over at the clock on the wall. When were they going to leave?—it was already a quarter to nine.

"Would you like another sweater? You're shivering."

"Excuse me, what did you say?"

Stephen didn't answer; he was busy taking off his black pullover sweater. "Here," he said, handing it to her, "you're cold. Put it on."

"But what about you?" she asked, staring at his soft, rumpled, dark hair and the breadth of his shoulders under the plaid flannel shirt. "Won't you get cold?"

"No. Besides, I can always turn the heat up. The thermostat's right over there." Stephen got up and walked over to the far wall, bending over to read the temperature on the little metal box near the door.

Kip's taller, Missy thought to herself. But why was she comparing Kip to Stephen? Why should she care who was taller anyway?

Stephen walked back across the room and sat down in his chair, his hands gripping the knees of his faded jeans. He cleared his throat again and reached for the cider. "So, uhm, what do you like to do?" he asked, taking a gulp from his mug.

"Oh, I don't know—anything, everything."

"What would you be doing tonight, if you weren't here?"

"Oh, well, Kip—that's my boyfriend, Kip Morgan— and I were supposed to go over to Buffy's house."

"Buffy? Who's Buffy?"

"Oh, Buffy Sanders. Her real name's Barbara, but

everybody calls her Buffy. She goes with Tink Winslow—he's the vice-president of the junior class. Kip is the president. Kip and I were king and queen of the junior winter carnival, see, and..."

"And I suppose you were prince and princess at the homecoming dance?" Stephen said with a smirk.

"Yes," Missy said slowly, "how did you know?"

"I didn't. It just goes along with the rest of the picture."

"What picture?" Missy asked, a bit indignant at Stephen's rather haughty attitude.

"Oh, Buffy, Tink, Kip, the winter carnival, the class president; it all just fits together," Stephen commented, leaning back in his chair and closing his eyes.

"Well," Missy began defensively, "didn't they have dances and class presidents at your old school in Boston?"

Stephen opened one eye and stretched out his arms. "Oh, I suppose so," he said, yawning, "but none of my friends ever paid any attention to all of that preppy business."

"Well, excuse me for boring you! And what did you and your friends think was worth your attention?" Missy asked, sitting forward on the couch.

"Well, in the first place all of my friends have normal names—not things like Ducky and Plucky and Wink."

"That's *Tink*, not Wink," Missy shouted at him, getting up from the sofa and standing in front of his chair. "What makes you think that you can make fun of my friends like that? You don't even know them! Just wait till the first day of school. You'll find out who Kip Morgan and Buffy Sanders and Tink Winslow are, and you'll wish you hadn't said all of these awful things to me. You'll just be begging Kip for his friendship. Why, any guy who's a friend of Kip's is set for life at Highland High!" Missy caught her breath and brushed back a lock of hair that had worked its way out of the blue grosgrain ribbon that served as a headband.

"You have beautiful hair," Stephen said quietly, looking up at her.

"Oh, don't try to make up for all of the damage you've done," Missy answered sharply. Suddenly the door opened and Mrs. McRae appeared.

"Is everything all right in here?" she asked hesitantly. "I thought I heard some rather loud voices coming from this room. Stephen, are you giving Missy a hard time?"

"No, no—everything's fine, Mom. Missy was just telling me about Highland High, and I was telling her about *Rainbow* at Mount Auburn High."

"Oh, yes, *Rainbow*. That was the literary magazine at Stephen's old school. He was just a sophomore when they made him assistant editor. I suppose had we stayed, he'd be the editor this year." Mrs. McRae beamed. Stephen's cheeks were beginning to redden again.

"It's hard to move to a new place, Missy, especially when you're in high school. Stephen's father and I are so glad you could come over tonight so that at least he'll know some names and a friendly face when he goes to school on Tuesday," she added before she rejoined her guests in the living room, satisfied that all was well in the den.

"Oh, I'll know a whole bunch of names," Stephen began once his mother left. "There's Bink, and Scruffy, and Kip, and the smiling face of Missy Cartwright underneath her homecoming crown."

Missy felt the blood rush through her veins and a burst of heat explode underneath the two sweaters she was wearing over her blouse. His sweater! She was wearing this obnoxious creep's sweater! Quickly she pulled the sweater over her head and threw it back at Stephen. "You really are too rude for words," Missy seethed, lowering her voice so as not to alert Mrs. McRae. "I didn't want to come over here tonight. I would much rather have spent the evening with my friends, yes *my* friends with their preppy names and class offices and homecoming crowns. And if you don't like all of that, Stephen McRae, you can take your clarinet, and your rainbows, and your yawns and snide remarks and pack them off to Boston." Missy got up from the sofa and began to head for the door when Stephen called her name. "What?" she said angrily, turning around to find him facing her.

"You're terrific," he said quietly, the sarcastic smile gone from his face.

Missy just stood there, caught off guard by this remark, until she finally regained her composure. "Thanks," she murmured, unable to return the compliment, then leaving to join her parents in the living room.

"We were just getting ready to come and get you," her mother said as Missy joined her on the couch. "It's getting late and you have a dentist's appointment at nine tomorrow morning, so we'd best be on our way. Did you fill Stephen in on Highland Park?"

Missy just nodded, noticing Stephen standing in the

archway that led from the dining room to the living room, eating an apple and watching her intently.

"So Stephen, do you have a pretty good idea what to expect on Tuesday?" his father asked him, walking toward the hall closet to get out the Cartwrights' coats.

"Oh yes," Stephen answered, taking another bite of his apple, his green eyes never moving from their scrutiny of Missy's face. "I know exactly what to expect."

Unable to bear his gaze any longer, Missy closed her eyes and turned around, opening them only when she was sure she wouldn't find Stephen's face. She walked around the opposite side of the couch from the doorway where he stood, and went into the hallway where Mr. McRae was holding her coat. She shivered as she slid her arms into the coat sleeves, and pulled the coat tightly around her, tugging the hat way down on her head and knotting the scarf at her neck.

"Your scarf matches your eyes," Stephen said quietly, having joined her in the hallway. "You know what they should call that color?"

"What?" she said, expecting yet another wisecrack.

Stephen leaned forward, close to her ear. "Melissa blue," he whispered.

Missy swallowed and stepped back, away from him. A funny feeling began in her stomach and rose up into her chest, a lightness halfway between a giggle and a hiccup. Kip never even noticed the color of her scarf. "That's a nice thing to say," she said softly, not certain how to respond to such words, and glad to see her mother and father coming into the hallway.

"I'm so glad we're all together again," Mrs. Cartwright said as her family prepared to brave once again the Chicago winter.

"So am I," Frank McRae agreed, "and maybe the kids can carry this friendship on into the next generation."

Neither Missy nor Stephen repsonded to that remark, but both exchanged polite goodnights, and Stephen joined his parents at the window as they watched the Cartwrights make their way through the snowdrifts toward their house.

By the time they were on their own front porch the Cartwrights were covered with a soft blanket of the heavy, wet snowflakes.

"Hurry, Daddy, open the door," Missy called out, her teeth chattering as Mr. Cartwright turned the key in the lock.

Inside, they quickly took off their things and began to hang them on the coat racks.

"Are you still planning to call Kip, honey? It's gotten pretty late," her mother said as she unzipped her own boots and put them on the rubber mat next to the door.

Missy thought for a moment before she answered. "No, I'll just talk to him tomorrow," she said as she took off her soaking hat.

"Such a pretty hat and scarf, Miss, and they look so good on you. You were lucky to find a set in that color," her mother said as she walked down the hall.

"Melissa blue," Missy whispered to herself as she hung the hat and scarf on the rack to dry, and walked slowly up the stairs to get ready for bed.

Two

"HELLO, KIP. Come on in. Missy's still upstairs, but she'll be down in a minute," Mrs. Cartwright said as she opened the back door and let Kip into the warm kitchen filled with the smell of brewing coffee and cinnamon toast. "Would you like a slice of toast and some milk while you wait?"

Kip shook his head and sat down in a kitchen chair, his long legs stretched out in front of him until his lace-up booted feet almost reached the chairs on the opposite side of the blond wooden table. "No, thanks, Mrs. C. My mom goes bananas with breakfast on the first day of school, so I'm full up. She thinks I'll starve between now and lunch hour unless I have half the food in the fridge inside of me before I leave the house. You should've seen the table this morning. Food City."

Mrs. Cartwright laughed as she set a glass of milk at Missy's place and then went to the oven to take out the hot pieces of cinnamon toast. As the spicy smell wafted toward Kip, his wide-set gray eyes grew large. Trying to hold back a smile, Mrs. Cartwright asked him if he had changed his mind about eating while he waited.

"Well, now that you mention it, I think there's one little spot that still isn't completely filled," he answered sheepishly. "Are you sure there's enough?"

"Believe me," Mrs. Cartwright told him, "I learned soon enough when Jim was your age that if a mother expects to have teenagers, especially boys, in her house, she'd better keep the refrigerator full at all times." As she watched Kip devour the two slices of bread without even pausing between them, she quickly turned to face the kitchen sink so that Kip wouldn't see her amusement.

The light, rapid footsteps on the staircase signaled Missy's arrival, and Kip looked up to see her racing into the kitchen, her cheeks flushed with excitement.

"Kip! I didn't know that you had come yet—Mom, why didn't you tell me Kip was here! Boy, look at the time. We'd better run, or else we won't make the bus. I sure don't want to be late today," she chattered, in between gulps of the milk. She stood back for a minute in front of Kip, waiting for him to comment on the outfit she had chosen especially for him.

"Well, if we're in such a hurry, why are you just standing there? Come on, Miss, get your coat. Tink and the others are going to be waiting for us, so we'd better get a move on." Kip noticed a shadow of disappointment cross Missy's face. "What's the matter, Mistletoe, d'you drink your milk too fast?"

"Don't you notice anything different?" she asked quietly, looking down at the floor.

"Uhh, oh, yeah, you, uhh, parted your hair in the center this morning. Looks nice, Miss," Kip said quickly.

"Oh, Kippy—I always wear my hair parted in the center!" she told him huffily, and stormed out of the kitchen to get her coat from the closet. "Boy," Missy said to herself out loud, "Buffy and I spend half the day at the Mall on Saturday trying to find the right jacket to go with my new wine corduroy pants, and does he notice a thing? Oh, no, that would be too much trouble for Kenneth Harrington Morgan III. Does he tell me that the wine-colored border on the collar of my blouse goes exactly with the pants, and that the navy blue blazer is the perfect complement? Does he notice that I'm wearing the elephant-hair bracelet he gave me for my birthday last year? Or that I got new stud earrings with hand-painted flowers on a blue enamel background? Does he even notice that the ribbon in my hair is tied in a bow instead of knotted underneath my hair in the back because he told me once that girls look really cute with bows in their hair? No, not Kip Morgan! All he finds to say is that I'm wearing my hair parted in the center today—which is the way I've been wearing it since the very first day he met me!"

Missy pulled on her coat and swung the scarf around her neck, not even bothering with her hat, which she jammed into her coat pocket. She marched back into the kitchen, picked up her bookbag and purse and glared at Kip. "Come on, let's go. I thought you said you were ready."

"What did I do?" he asked Mrs. Cartwright, holding up his hands and turning from Missy to face her mother.

"Oh, no," Mrs. Cartwright said quickly, "you're not pulling me into this. Don't you want something for breakfast before you go, dear?"

"Not hungry," Missy said shortly. "I'll just take a yogurt and eat it on the way," she said, opening the refrigerator and taking out a small carton of strawberry yogurt. She opened the drawer near the sink and took a white plastic spoon from the stack Mrs. Cartwright kept there for such emergencies.

"You mean you're going to eat that walking down the street?" Kip asked her as they went out the door and down the walk toward the alley behind the house.

"Sure," Missy answered, her breath misty white in the cold morning air. She removed the plastic lid and licked the yogurt off before she dumped the lid in the trash can behind the Cartwrights' house. "Why?"

Kip shook his head at her. "Not cool, Miss. Not cool at all. What if somebody sees you?"

"So?" she asked, stirring the fruit up into the creamy white yogurt.

"So? So everything! You're my girl, Miss, and I have an image to protect. It just isn't cool to walk down the street eating a carton of yogurt, that's all. You should be able to figure that out. You look like a leftover from the hippies. Next thing I know you'll be passing out flowers and incense in airports. Can't you do something with that stuff before we get to the bus stop?"

Missy tried to eat the yogurt as fast as she could, but between being upset over Kip's disregard for her outfit, and the cold air, and the simple fact that it's almost impossible to eat when someone is rushing you, the yogurt stuck like a blob of glue in her throat.

"C'mon, Missy—we're almost there!"

Missy threw the plastic spoon at Kip's feet and glared at him, her eyes filling with tears. "You're making me nuts, Kip, stop it. You've been at me ever since you came over this morning. Can't I do anything right?"

Kip bent down and picked up the spoon, dusting it off with the sleeve of his dark green hunting jacket. He handed it back to Missy who shook her head, refusing to take it. They stood there for a moment, Kip looking at Missy, the spoon held out in his hand, and Missy looking down at the snow, a slow trickle of tears falling from her eyes. Finally Kip reached out with his other arm and pulled Missy toward him, even though she tried to shrug him away.

"Don't cry, Missy," Kip told her, putting both arms around her, still holding the spoon in his right hand.

Missy kept her arms at her sides but allowed herself to be enfolded in Kip's strong, warm hug.

"It's all right, Miss—I didn't mean to get you all upset, honest. I wouldn't do that, Missy. I wouldn't try to make you cry."

"Well, then, why didn't you notice my new blazer?" Missy asked him, raising her tear-stained face from his shoulder and looking up into his gray eyes. She sniffed back the tears that felt frozen on her face, and wiped the tip of her red nose with the back of her hand.

"Miss, guys don't notice things like that. Blazers or new skirts or a pair of shoes."

"Some guys do," she told him quietly.

"Well, maybe some guys talk about it more than I do, but all I know is that you're the most beautiful girl I've ever seen, and you looked as great this morning as you always do. You know I think you're beautiful, don't you, Miss? I mean, geez, we're the best looking couple in the school. I'm proud to show you off to the other guys."

"You are?" Missy asked, slightly disturbed by this remark but not really sure why.

"You bet! We're a great team, Missy. I mean, we've got the whole school at our feet."

"I know," Missy agreed. "Half the girls in the school are in love with you, Kippy."

Kip smiled broadly, his even, white teeth shining against the rosy, clear skin of his face. With one brown-gloved hand he brushed back a stray wisp of Missy's hair from her forehead and ran his thumb down the side of her face. "You're so beautiful, Mistletoe, so perfect for me. That's why I get upset when you do crazy things like wearing that old purple skirt to school two days before homecoming, or talking about cutting your hair, or eating yogurt on the street. I mean, when you can be perfect—and I mean perfect—as you were on the night of the winter carnival, well... When I saw you come down the stairs in that blue dress, your hair all fixed up, you know, in those soft curls, wearing the locket I gave you for last Valentine's Day, I just knew that we'd win as king and queen. All I could think about was how our picture would look in the paper next week, you and I, wearing the crowns and sitting up on the stage. Remember that first king and queen dance, where they lowered the lights and only the two of us were allowed on the floor? You know what I was think-ing? I thought, every guy in this room wishes he was me, that he was king of this carnival and that Missy was his girl. And you knew that all the girls were wishing they were you. Everyone watching us, every-one wishing to be us. That's what we've got, Miss, we're a great team, Mistletoe—when are you going to realize it?"

Missy looked into his eyes and nodded her head. "I do realize it, Kip. And I do know how lucky I am—how lucky we are. It's just that sometimes I think you expect too much of me; that you expect me always to be perfect, never to have a zit on my face, never to wear an outfit that isn't perfect prep. I mean, I can't be perfect all the time."

"Yes, you can, Missy," he answered firmly, "you can." Kip slid his fingers under her chin and lifted her face up toward his own. Slowly he leaned toward her till she smelled the fresh scent of the soap he always used, that woodsy smell that reminded her of pine needles and spearmint. She felt his warm mouth brush her lips, the soft lock of hair that fell from his neat side part gently skimming her own forehead. "We're the perfect couple, Miss," he whispered in her ear. "Kip and Missy—the absolute best."

He stepped back away from her, looking down into her face. "You still want this spoon?"

Missy shook her head. "No, I've had enough. We can throw it out in the Mitchells' garbage can," she said, handing him the yogurt carton.

Kip didn't answer but sprinted over to the trash cans lining the alley and dumped the yogurt in one of the open cans. He raced back to Missy's side and handed her his handkerchief. "Here, dry your eyes, beautiful. Can't have the winter queen showing up on the first day looking like a pink-eyed rabbit."

Missy laughed and wiped her eyes. "Oh, well, so much for the new light blue eyeshadow I put on this morning. I'll have to stop and fix my face when we get to school."

"Good idea," Kip said, taking her hand as they continued down the street. He squeezed her fingers affectionately, dropped her hand, and slung his whole arm around her shoulder. As they rounded the corner of their alley shortcut, they could see the big yellow school bus beginning to lumber down Chestnut Street.

"Come on, Missy—we've got to run for it," he shouted, dropping his arm and extending his hand to her.

She held on tightly as Kip ran slightly ahead of her, his long legs outdistancing her slower pace.

"Wait!" Kip yelled as the last two students prepared to board the bus. "Wait for us."

The bus driver saw them coming and held the bus until they arrived, breathless, at the door. "You kids ought to leave yourselves more time to get here," he scolded as they hurried aboard.

They moved on into the bus, greeting friends, and looking for a roomy space amidst the crowds of their fellow students.

Kip caught his breath and bent down to whisper in Missy's ear. "We can't be late like this again. It's not exactly cool to have to run for the bus and then get on all out of breath and a wreck. Definitely uncool, Miss. No more scenes from now on, okay?"

"Okay," Missy nodded, struggling to tie a proper bow in the ribbon that had come undone. She sighed as the bus lurched forward, carrying its riders toward the first day of the new semester.

Three

"THIS SEMESTER we'll be concentrating on American literature," Ms. McFadden announced. The class was busily copying down the various names and dates she had written on the blackboard. "The other junior English classes will be reading a mixture of different books this semester, some American, some British, and some translations of a couple of the European classics. But your reading list will consist of only American literature books. Honors English students should have one solid year of American studies, so this semester will be a continuation of the last one. Most of you were here last semester; in fact only Stephen McRae," she said, indicating Stephen, who had chosen a seat in the back row near the windows, "is new to this class. But I'm sure that having gone to the school he did in Boston, he'll have no trouble adjusting. Perhaps one of you could meet with Stephen after class and give him an idea of the kinds of things we did last semester," Mrs.

McFadden said as the bell sounded. "Okay, that's it for today. For tomorrow, I'd like you all to have at least begun Hawthorne's "Custom House Introduction" to *The Scarlet Letter.* You can't really understand *The Scarlet Letter* unless you've given "The Custom House" a thorough going-over. Well, see you tomorrow," she said as the class scrambled for their books and headed for the doorway.

Missy reached under her chair for her notebook and saw a shadow cross her desk. Without even looking up she knew who was standing there.

"Hello, friendly face," Stephen's voice said.

She looked up at him, puzzled. "What?"

"Remember? My mother said I'd know at least one friendly face when I got to school on Tuesday, and I was just bidding it hello," he smiled.

Were his eyes that green the other night? Missy wondered. Like the bright, fresh leaves of a forest, Stephen's clear green eyes shone against the smooth, healthy glow of his skin. He was wearing the same black pullover sweater he had lent her the other night, with a crisp white shirt underneath and a pair of comfortable, faded jeans. His whole face radiated energy, and Missy wasn't sure whether the excitement she was suddenly feeling was simply due to first-day-of-school-jitters, or to the fact that Stephen had the ability to unnerve her slightly.

"Uhm, is everything going okay for you?" she asked politely.

"Oh, great. I tried out for the orchestra second period, and was accepted on the spot, so everything else is unimportant. Except for this class, of course."

"Oh, that's right," Missy answered, nodding her

head, "you like to write. I suppose you must like books, then. It sort of follows."

"Sort of does," Stephen said, laughing. He paused for a moment, studying her intently, and then cleared his throat before he began to speak. "Is there any color that doesn't look wonderful on you?" he asked softly.

Missy felt the corners of her mouth begin to curl in a smile, but she looked down at her desk and played with the end of wire that was jutting out from her spiral ring notebook. "Oh, uh, I don't ever wear too much purple. It's not the best color one can pick."

"Oh, I bet you'd look wonderful in purple. Like a wild iris or a violet."

Missy looked up at him, and found herself again without words.

"Are you going to lunch now?" Stephen asked her. "If you've got fifth period lunch too, maybe we could eat together and then you could fill me in on all of the stuff I missed in here last semester." He was quiet for a moment, as if he were not quite sure he should say what was on his mind. He took a deep breath and then added, "Somehow I didn't quite expect to find you in this class, Melissa."

"Why not? English has always been my best subject. Why shouldn't I be in the Honors class?"

"Somehow it doesn't all fit with the things you told me about yourself the other night," he answered. "I have this bad habit of making hasty judgments about people, oh, from the way they look, that sort of thing. I've tried to become more broad-minded and take each person as an individual, not expecting any particular thing, not looking for any pattern. But I guess I'm still guilty of jumping to conclusions."

"And what sort of conclusions did you jump to about me?"

Stephen smiled sheepishly. "That you didn't care much about school; I figured you were only interested in clothes and parties, that sort of thing."

"Well, I am interested in clothes and parties. *And* in my schoolwork. I told you the other night—I'm interested in everything." Missy stood up and took her shoulder bag from the back of her desk chair where she had hung it. She began to walk toward the door, Stephen following close behind. "Do you know your way to the cafeteria?" she asked him.

"I suppose I can find it by myself if I have to—but I'd rather go with you. That is, if you're free."

"Well..." Missy hesitated, "I usually have lunch with the same crowd every day, and they're sort of waiting for me down there. Umm, the table is usually crowded, but I suppose since it is your first day...I guess it would be okay if you sat at our table. We're over on the left side, right near the fruit machine. I've got to meet...a friend...at my locker, but I'll see you down there, okay?"

"Sure," Stephen answered, smiling, "over on the left, near the fruit machine—whatever that is."

"Oh, don't they have those in Boston? I'm sorry, I just assumed everybody had lunchrooms with those vending machines that sell apples and oranges...you know, like the ones that have candy."

"Okay, see you underneath the oranges," Stephen called as he went down the hall toward the staircase.

Missy turned away and raced toward her own locker two floors upstairs. Kip will be waiting, and he won't like this new situation one bit, she thought. Well, maybe if I explain that it's Stephen's first day, and that his parents are friends with my... She rounded the corner of the third floor stairwell to find Kip leaning against her locker, looking annoyed. He made a point of looking at his watch. "Nice, Missy—only ten minutes late. What were you doing, erasing the blackboards for McFadden?"

"No, no," she said, spinning the combination of her lock, "nothing like that. Are Buffy and Tink going to save the table?"

"Don't be dense. Nobody would dare to sit at that table, Miss. Everybody knows that that space belongs to The Group—even if the two main figures in The Group only have five seconds left at lunch to cram a tuna sandwich down their respective throats."

"Oh, Kip, don't make such a fuss over everything. We have plenty of time. Just let me get my French book and then we can go." She checked her hair in the small mirror she had hung on the inner door of her locker, and sprayed a light mist of "Heaven Scent" on both her wrists. "Okay, I'm all set."

"Finally," Kip muttered, taking her books from her and caryying them along with his own.

"You know, I'm quite capable of carrying my own books," Missy complained. She never liked it when Kip carried her books—it made her feel silly not having anything to do with her hands.

"I want to carry them," Kip insisted. "Then there's no doubt about who belongs to whom."

Before Missy could reply to Kip's remark, they had already reached the cafeteria and she would have had to shout to be heard over the accompanying din.

"There they are, all assembled, waiting for the king

and queen," Kip shouted. "Come on, Missy, this is our big entrance."

"Kip," Missy scolded, shaking her head at him. Every now and then Kip took his status as class president a bit too seriously and it bothered her. Maybe he'll simmer down once the first day of school is over, she thought as their friends called out to greet them.

"Here, you and Missy sit over on this side. That way she can talk to Buffy and I can talk to you," Tink told them.

"Ooh, Missy, I love your earrings," Poodie Hawkins cried. "Did you get them at Fairchild's?"

"No," Buffy interrupted, "we got them on Saturday at Field's. Aren't they the absolute best?"

"The best," Poodie agreed. "Did they have them in any other color than blue?"

"Mmm, I think they had some with pink flowers on a white background, didn't they, Buff?"

Buffy, whose mouth was already full of tuna fish sandwich, could only nod in agreement.

Missy took out her brown-bag lunch and unwrapped the peanut butter and apple on whole wheat that she had made earlier that morning.

"Whatcha got, Miss?" Kip asked, inspecting the contents of her lunch. "Oh, the same old macrobiotic mess, as usual," he laughed, a bit embarrassed. "Missy sort of goes in for natural foods, I guess," he apologized.

"Well, not me," Poodie declared, shaking her head. "I've been eating the same pineapple cream cheese on white sandwiches since seventh grade, and I don't intend to start eating a bunch of farm food now. I think an all-white sandwich looks...classic."

"Classic, that's a new one," Missy groaned as she bit

into her own sandwich. "Can we all just eat in peace this once without everybody jumping on me and telling me that I've brought yet another grievous lunch?"

"You said it, Miss, not me," Kip said, laughing and looking over at her sandwich. "Grievous."

"And speaking of grievous, who is this unlikely element approaching our sacred table," Tink asked, looking over Missy's shoulder at the figure who had just walked up behind her.

"Melissa?" Stephen said, and at the sound of his voice Missy whipped around to face him.

"Oh, Stephen, that's right. Uh, I see you found our table."

"Stephen? Melissa? What is this, Sunday school?" Win Winthrop said, tossing back a falling lock of his blond hair with a jerk of his head. "Who is this clown?"

Things were going badly already, and Missy knew that if she didn't save the situation immediately, it would be all over for Stephen then and there.

"Clown?" Stephen said before Missy had a chance to take control.

"Uhm, Win, Kip, Tink ... this is Stephen McRae from Boston."

"If he's from Boston, what's he doing here?" Poodie asked, giggling.

"I just moved here from Boston," Stephen told her politely.

"Yes, Stephen just moved here from Boston, and his parents are friends of my parents, and I asked him to join us at our lunch table today," Missy said, rushing to get the whole sentence out before someone else interrupted her.

"Your parents and his parents, huh? Was this the

guy whose house your parents dragged you to when you should have been watching *Superman II* at Buffy's with us?" Tink asked, looking Stephen up and down from head to foot. "You'd better watch it, Kip. Looks like you've got some heavy competition."

Stephen turned bright red, and Kip leaned back in his chair, a look of great annoyance clouding his face. Competition was one subject Kip Morgan did not take lightly.

"There's no room at the table, Missy," Kip announced.

"Well, uhm, if Tish and Jimbo move down that way a little," Missy said, pointing to the red-haired girl at the outer end of the table and her boyfriend, the star quarterback of the football team, who was sitting across from her, "then we could all squeeze over a bit and there would be room for one more chair. It'll be a little crowded, I'll admit, but if Tish just..."

"There's no room at this table, Missy," Kip repeated, emphatically, looking directly into Missy's eyes.

Missy tried to avoid Kip's angry glare; she was too embarrassed to face Stephen.

"Maybe I'd better just eat somewhere else," Stephen said quietly.

"No, that's not..." Missy began, trying to smooth things over, not wanting to send Stephen away to eat by himself, but not really strong enough to defy Kip in front of the whole crowd.

"As I said, there's no room at this table," Kip told them once again, his gaze never leaving Missy's face.

She looked into Kip's huge gray eyes trying to find a bit of understanding, a hint of compromise, but all she found was an iron will that could not give an inch.

"Is this going to be a repeat of the yogurt scene this morning?" Kip murmured so that only Missy could hear him.

She was not acting perfectly right now—the look in Kip's eyes told her that. "No," she mumbled, "no repeats. Stephen," she said, turning toward him but avoiding his eyes, "maybe it would be best, since there isn't much room..."

Stephen just nodded, the wounded look on his face telling her that he understood completely—Kip had just vetoed Stephen's acceptance into The Group, and Missy had gone along with the decision.

Without saying another word Stephen turned on his heel and walked away from the table, disappearing into the throng that clustered around the entrance to the food line.

Missy looked down at the uneaten sandwich that lay on the brown bag in front of her place. Her appetite was gone. Maybe she could have said something to ease the situation. Maybe she could have made some gesture that would have removed the hurt look from Stephen's eyes. She closed her eyes and swallowed hard. Stephen's face, the look of disappointment overshadowing the brightness of his eyes, rose up in her mind.

"Well, that takes care of that problem," Kip's voice boomed, breaking the silence that had fallen over the table.

"Ooh, I'm glad he's gone. He sort of gave me the creeps," Poodie giggled.

"Yeah, I doubt whether he'll tackle The Group anymore. Good work, Kipper," Tink said, laughing.

"Thank you, my man," Kip answered, joining in

the returning good humor that was sweeping over the table.

"I'm going to get an ice cream sandwich. Anybody else want anything?" Jimbo asked, hoisting his massive frame out of the chair.

Missy opened her eyes and looked around at her friends. Were someone to pass by the table who hadn't witnessed the incident with Stephen, he would never guess that anything out of the ordinary had happened this noon. But something has happened here, Missy thought; something that should not have taken place. What was going on with her since Stephen arrived in Highland Park? She had never before questioned Kip's judgment. If Kip told her she had made a grievous mistake, she accepted his pronouncement and tried to behave more correctly in the future. After all, if anybody knew his way around Highland Park, it was Kip Morgan.

But what he just did to Stephen was wrong, a voice within her said—Stephen's first day at Highland Park and Kip the president of the junior class. So Stephen isn't the preppiest guy in the world, so what? Kip and The Group should have welcomed him just to show what great guys they all are, just to prove that they are The Greatest. But they didn't; they made him feel even more of an outsider than he really is, more of a stranger. More alone.

And you didn't do a thing to stop them, Melissa Anne Cartwright, the voice continued. You could have—you could have insisted that there was room at the table, or gotten up and left with him when the others made him go. But you didn't, the voice said again. You just sat there and let him get hurt.

"But my place is here with Kip," Missy said out loud.

"What's that?" Kip said, looking over at her and smiling. "You say something, Mistletoe? You've been awfully quiet the last few minutes."

"Nothing important," Missy said, embarrassed that she had spoken out loud without even realizing it.

"Listen, Miss, I've got to go to a junior cabinet meeting after school in room 208," Kip told her, putting his arm around her shoulder, "so don't wait for me, okay?"

"Okay, Kip," she answered, snuggling deeper into the crook of his arm.

Everything will be all right, Missy thought as she sat there with Kip's arm around her, protecting her, making sure she was perfect. Everything will be just fine, she told herself, as long as I just listen to Kip.

From the corner of her eye she saw a black-sweatered figure get up from a far table, put his tray on the conveyor belt, and throw his trash in the garbage can. He paused for a moment near the door that led out of the cafeteria and looked over at the table where The Group was sitting, glancing at Kip with his arm around Missy. Missy closed her eyes, hoping that when she opened them Stephen would be gone.

She counted to ten and opened her eyes.

There was no one standing near the door.

Four

"THIS HAS really been a long day," Missy told Buffy as they walked from the assembly hall to their lockers. "I still don't know why they have to end the day with an upper-class assembly. After two weeks of Christmas vacation it's hard enough to get used to school again, let alone having to sit through an assembly before you go home. Boy, the principal sure needs help planning things around here."

"Yeah," Buffy answered, unwrapping a stick of gum and popping it in her mouth, "and I'm starving. During vacation, I kind of got used to going to the refrigerator all day. No wonder I don't fit into my gym suit. Oh, Missy, do you think there'll ever be a time when I won't have to diet?"

Missy smiled and shrugged her shoulders. "Who knows, by the time we're thirty maybe some terrific doctor will have found some way to let people eat all they want without gaining weight. Or maybe they'll

find a way to take the calories out of food. That's it—
you're good at science, Buff. Why don't you become a
famous scientist and find a cure for fat!"

Buffy laughed and shook her head at Missy. "You're
really lame, Cartwright. Sometimes I worry about
you." Buffy spun her combination lock, opened her
locker, and threw her books inside. "I'd walk to the bus
with you, but I promised my mom I'd meet her on Lawn-
dale Avenue. We've got to get a birthday present for
my sister. I'll call you tonight after supper, okay?
Maybe you can come over and show me how to do that
thing where you weave the ribbons through the barrettes."

"Sure," Missy said, rummaging around on the floor
of her locker, trying to locate a mitten. "I've got a little
French to do, but since Kip is busy, I'll have time to do
it now, so I'll be free tonight. Call about 7:00, all right?"

"Right," Buffy said as she slammed her locker,
locked the lock, and went off down the hall. "See ya,"
she called over her shoulder.

"Yeah, see ya," Missy called back, still searching for
her glove. She knelt down on the cold, brown linoleum
floor and reached her arm up to the elbow into the
locker, feeling around in the back corner for her mitten.

"Digging for buried treasure?" a voice asked from
behind her.

She swiveled around on her knees to find Stephen
looking down at her. "Oh, it's you," she said, her cheeks
flushing as the incident at the lunch table once again
began to trouble her.

"Yes, only me," Stephen answered. "The Great Man
didn't wait to walk you home today?"

Missy looked down at the floor and didn't answer.

"Sorry," he said quickly, "I shouldn't have said that. I hope I didn't cause you any hassles with your friends at lunch. I shouldn't have intruded like that."

Missy stopped searching for her mitten and started to stand up when Stephen held out his hand to help her.

"Thanks," she said, as she rose to her feet. As soon as she was standing, she dropped his hand and turned back again to get her things from her locker. What a strong grip he has, her secret voice told her. What nice, warm hands. The only way to shut the voice up was to begin talking. "Oh, you don't have to apologize—I'm as much to blame as you are. Kip is, well, very protective of The Group, and he...uhh...he doesn't make friends very easily," she lied, trying to make Stephen feel better.

"Sure," Stephen smiled wickedly, "that's the way he became class president."

Missy bit her lower lip, ashamed for having tried to fool Stephen. He was far too clever to fall for such a ridiculous excuse.

"Good try, Melissa," Stephen admitted, and she had to laugh along with him. "Since it looks as though lunch is out for a while, are you free to walk home with me, or are you only allowed to walk with select members of The Almighty Group?" Stephen asked her as she put on her coat and began to search once more for the lost mitten.

"Don't be a dodo. I can walk home with anyone I choose."

"I don't mean to pry," Stephen said as she continued to plough through the notebooks and papers on the floor of her locker, "but what in the world are you searching for in there?"

"My mitten. I had it this morning when I left the house and now it's gone. There's only one here." She held out the remaining mitten and sighed.

"Oh, no—the 'Melissa blue' mitten that matches the 'Melissa blue' scarf that matches the 'Melissa blue' hat. Horrors, that mitten is priceless! Are you sure you didn't leave it at home?"

"No, I'm positive I wore it this morning," she lamented, slamming her locker and closing the lock. "I'm afraid it's gone for good."

"Nonsense, Watson," Stephen exclaimed, rubbing his thumb and finger along the imaginary beard on his chin. "This calls for a simple process by which we retrace all of the steps that Melissa, Melissa...what's your middle name anyway?"

"Anne"

"...The steps that Melissa Anne Cartwright took this morning which led to the disappearance of the object in question. Yes, Watson, you can call this case 'Study in Melissa Blue.' Come, Watson, the hour of decision is upon us."

Missy had no idea what Stephen was chattering on about, but she had seen enough old Sherlock Holmes movies to know that Dr. Watson was the famous detective's faithful assistant and biographer. She laughed as Stephen took a pair of wire-rimmed glasses out of his pocket, and held them in his hand with only one lens showing so that they resembled a magnifying glass. He turned toward her and without a trace of a smile on his face he bent down close to the ground as if to follow the trail that the mitten had left on the linoleum. "Aha!" he cried, and scooped up a piece of fuzz from the floor. "Look Watson, a clue!"

Missy couldn't stop laughing. "But that fuzz is red," she got out in between the laughter.

"Very devious, that Professor Moriarty. You see— he's kidnapped the Melissa Mitten, and has dyed this fragment of wool red just to throw us off the right course. Hurry, Watson, time is running out! That Moriarty is a devious fellow. If we don't find the mitten soon, who knows what the consequences may be. First one mitten, then a glove—who knows where Moriarty will stop. That's his plan—to freeze us all! Hurry, Watson—the month of January is just beginning!"

Stephen grabbed Melissa's hand and together they ran down the hall and through the door to the stairwell. They tore down the stairs into the courtyard, and then out onto the back lawn of the school.

"Is this the way you came to school?" Stephen whispered. "We must retrace your steps exactly."

"Uhh huh," Missy nodded, "I got off the bus over there near the driveway, and then walked up this way to the entrance over there on the side."

"Quickly, Watson, before one of Moriarty's henchmen spots us," Stephen commanded, and they raced over to the entrance where they began retracing Missy's steps all the way to the bus stop.

"It's gone for good," Missy said dejectedly when they reached the driveway. "I knew we wouldn't find it."

"Poppycock!" Stephen said.

"Poppycock?" Missy repeated.

Stephen began to chuckle. "I don't know what it means either, but they always say that in movies when somebody is about to give up and the movie won't be over for another half hour."

"You're really a case, Stephen McRae, you know that?" Missy laughed.

"Believe me, I've been called worse things than that," he replied. "But enough of this idle chitchat, Watson, here comes the bus."

"Maybe I lost it on the bus," Missy told Stephen as they climbed aboard and found two seats toward the back. Most of the crowd had left on the earlier buses, so there were few students now except for the stragglers, since those with afterschool activities wouldn't be getting out for another hour.

"You know, Highland Park is better than I expected," Stephen told her, looking out the window as the bus drove along the winding road that twisted and turned through the lush pine tree forests. "I thought that a suburb of Chicago would be all modern houses and asphalt roads without a tree or bird in sight. I can't believe that this place has these forests and Lake Michigan, and these great big old houses that border on the ravines."

"Oh, yes," Missy told him. "When Jimmy—that's my older brother—and I were little Mom and Dad wouldn't let us wander around too far from the house at night. They were afraid we'd get lost in the ravines and would never be found again."

"What's this?" Stephen asked as they drove past a huge gate with a sign that said "Ravinia" over the entrance.

"That's Ravinia Park. It's an open-air concert hall where the Chicago Symphony gives performances during the summer. My parents get tickets every year. I used to go with them a lot when I was younger, but Kip doesn't much like classical music, so we only go when they have pop concerts or an occasional rock band. It's really beautiful. If you can afford it—and can manage to get one—you can buy a ticket for a seat inside the actual band shell up front. But most people just bring blankets, get a general admission ticket and lie on the grass, listening to music and watching the stars come out. Sometimes my Mom packs a picnic supper and they get there early and have a feast on their blanket before the concert starts. There are some fancy restaurants way inside where you can get all dressed up and have dinner before the concert, but I've never been there."

"It sounds just like Tanglewood," Stephen remarked. "That's the same sort of place near Boston. My friends and I went there last summer. It was great because my best friend Mike got his driver's license and we drove over to Tanglewood with a bunch of the orchestra people from school. It was fantastic."

"Did you have a girlfriend in Boston?" Missy asked, not knowing whether she ought to pry, but curious, just the same.

Stephen continued to look out the window, his face taking on a faraway look. "Yeah, I had a girlfriend in Boston."

"Do you two still write?"

"It's complicated, see," he began. "Actually, she moved away last August—to California. Her father is a professor, and he got a new job out there, so the whole family had to move—just the way mine did when Dad got his new job in Chicago. For a while we wrote, but by about Thanksgiving the letters were getting fewer and fewer, and then with all the confusion about moving to Chicago—well, I'll probably never hear from her again."

"What's her name?"

"Lucy," he replied. "She's got long red hair and she plays the flute." Stephen was quiet for a moment, and just stared out the window, watching the continuous line of pine trees that rushed past them as the bus plunged on through the ravine. "Oh, well," he finally said, "ancient history."

The bus began to slow down and turned on to a broad street where the houses were set back from the road. "Come on," Missy said, tapping Stephen's arm, "we can get off here. There's a shortcut that Kip and I take through the alley. It's much quicker than waiting for the bus to weave up and down all the streets before it gets to the stop near my house." She jumped up and began to walk toward the door, Stephen following close behind her.

They got off the bus and began walking down the wide, snow-covered alley that snaked behind the back yards of the houses on the main street and was bordered by the ravines on the other side. The snow was beginning to fall again, and the sun had already left the sky, enfolding the woods in an early winter twilight. One evening star had already begun to shine in the smoky blue sky, and a thin, crescent moon hovered over the steeple of a nearby church.

Suddenly Stephen grabbed Missy's elbow. "Look—over there! Victory!" he shouted, pointing to a patch of snow a few feet from the garbage cans behind the Mitchells' house.

"What?"

"There, Watson—look!"

Lying half-buried in newfallen snow was the mitten that had dropped from Missy's pocket during her argument with Kip over the yogurt.

Stephen raced over and bent down, retrieving the mitten and dusting off the powdery snow that covered it. "Your glove, my lady," he said, as he walked over to her and offered her the mitten, bowing from the waist. "The 'Study in Melissa Blue' comes to an end."

"Thanks, thanks so much," she answered as she shook out the mitten and slid it onto her freezing hand. "Nice work, Sherlock," she added gaily.

"My pleasure, Watson," he answered, enormously pleased with his own success.

They walked on together toward Missy's street, talking about the things that had gone on in Honors English first semester, about the books the class had read, and about how everyone agreed that Ms. McFadden was the best teacher any of them had ever had.

"She's the sponsor of the literary magazine. If you like to write stories, you should talk to her about writing something for *Wordsmith*. If you write something for the magazine and they accept it, then you're automatically a member of the literary guild."

"Have you ever written anything?" he asked.

"No, I don't have the time to write. I've thought up ideas for a couple of stories, but there always seems to be something that I have to do before I can sit down and write my story, so it just never gets written."

"What sort of things do you do instead?"

"Well, I remember one time," Missy began, and then stopped herself. "Oh, this sounds silly. I've never told anybody about my dumb ideas for stories," she said, blushing.

"No, no, go ahead. I want to hear about your story," Stephen told her eagerly.

"I had this idea," she began again, looking down at the ground and pushing the snow back and forth with the toe of her boot, "about, oh—it was too silly, never mind," she said quickly, and started to walk again.

"You don't have to tell me," he said gently, "sometimes it's hard to talk about an idea for a story. I just wondered why you didn't try to write it."

"It was the weekend before homecoming, and Kip and I were in charge of the junior class float, and I was too busy to do anything other than paste crepe paper sheets over chicken wire," she told Stephen. "And then I had to get my dress for the dance fixed—it was too loose around the waist and Mom had to take it in—and Buffy and I looked all over town for earrings that would match the locket that Kip gave me for Valentine's Day and which I wanted to wear with my dress. And then, the night before the dance, Kip decided to give a "float building party" in his back yard, and I stayed up too late, so that by the time the dance rolled around I had such a headache I had to take two aspirins and lie down before I got dressed to go. But it was a wonderful dance. Since Kip and I are only juniors we couldn't be in the running for homecoming king and queen, but the prince and princess are always juniors, and of course Kip won as prince—he always wins everything around Highland High. It's amazing. I mean, sometimes I can't believe that of all the girls in the school that he could choose, I was the one Kip picked."

Stephen just looked at Missy and shook his head. "Why can't you believe it? Kip should feel lucky that you wanted him—you've got it all backwards."

"Oh, no," Missy said, shaking her head, "you don't understand. You'll see when you've been around Highland longer. Kip Morgan is The Person around school. Even some of the seniors look up to Kip, and that's almost unheard of. Every girl in that school would give anything to go out with Kip. I can't explain it. It's not only that he's so good-looking, or that he's always so together, it's more than that. He always knows the right thing to do, he's never tripping over himself, or stumbling for words, or doing anything that would make him look like a jerk. All he has to do is smile, and every girl in the room goes crazy. And see, when I'm with Kip, I have that magic, too. He knows all the rules, and if I'm about to do something dopey, he's there to tell me, to protect me. Without Kip, I'd be..."

"Fantastic," Stephen said quietly.

"Hardly," Missy said. "I know that the reason The Group was so willing to accept me was all Kip's doing. You see, I went to a different junior high school than they did because we lived in a different house and I was in another school district before. Kip had another girlfriend back then, but he broke up with her when he met me. He sat behind me in study hall, and he used to call me "Blondie." I'd never met anybody like Kip before. I'd had some dates, and I always had lots of friends, but the minute Kip started to notice me, my whole life changed. Suddenly I was somebody that everyone wanted to know. The first party he took me to I was so nervous I almost spilled a Coke all over Tink's mother's yellow rug. But Kip was cool, and took care of me, and made sure that everyone was nice to me. And little by little I realized that people were seeking me out, that my name was turning up on ballots

for dance princesses, for the chairperson of clothes
drives for last year's service club benefit, in the school
newspaper as someone to watch.

"I remember once I wore an embroidered ribbon in
my hair—really pretty ribbon with these blue and violet flowers and butterflies—and a few days later half
the girls in my class had gone out and bought that same
ribbon, and were wearing it in their hair. It was amazing. And then to be crowned queen of the winter carnival—well, I kept wondering when I was going to
wake up and find that I was dreaming. My picture was
in both the school newspaper and the *Highland Park
Gazette,* and everybody asked me before the dance what
I was planning to wear, and Kip brought me the most
beautiful orchid corsage—I still have it pressed in the
phone book in my room. And then, when he and I were
crowned, they presented me with this huge bouquet of
long-stemmed, dark red roses and put this crown on
my head, and Kip was crowned too, and everyone was
applauding." Missy paused to catch her breath. "I was
so nervous and excited, my head pounded for a week.
Everyone was watching me, so I couldn't blow it. But
Kip was always there, by my side, telling me how to
act, and what not to do, so I made it through just fine.
Kip says we're sure to be crowned king and queen of
the April Showers dance this spring, and Buffy agrees
with him. I don't know if I can take all that again,
though," she said, laughing and running her hands
over her face.

Stephen just stood there looking at her, saying nothing. Finally he spoke up. "Don't you ever just want to
do what *you* want to do—not what Kip and The Group
expect you to do?"

Missy looked at him, puzzled. "But I am doing what I want to do. I'm doing what *every* girl wants to do!"

"Maybe," Stephen said, shrugging his shoulders, "but I'm not altogether convinced."

"What are you talking about? Who could have more than I do?" Missy asked him, dismayed.

"Nobody, I guess—if you've got what you really want."

"Of course I do," she insisted, "I've got what everybody wants."

"I didn't ask you if you've got what everybody wants; I asked you if you've got what Melissa Anne Cartwright wants."

"How'd you remember my middle name?" she asked, startled.

"I remember everything you tell me," Stephen answered, "everything."

Missy smiled at him, and shook her head. "You're full of surprises, Stephen, Stephen...what's your middle name?"

Stephen made an awful face. "I never reveal my middle name—it's too terrible for words."

"Oh, come on," she teased, "it can't be that bad. Kip's middle name is Harrington. Kenneth Harrington Morgan III."

"Well, my middle name sure isn't herringbone, and I'm not about to tell you what it is either. I must preserve my air of mystery—you know, the stranger who came out of the great Northeast—the stranger whose middle name she never knew."

Missy began to laugh and started up the path that led to the Cartwrights' back yard. "Listen, stranger from the Northeast, I've got to help my mom get dinner ready. Can you find your way back to your house from here? If you just cut through those trees over there, you'll be on Maple Street, okay?"

"Do you doubt the navigational powers of the great Inspector McRae?" Stephen asked, grinning. "Ah, how quickly they forget," he muttered as he began walking toward Maple Street. "I'll see you tomorrow in English," he called out, walking backward so that he could face her.

"Yeah, see ya," she called out as she ran happily through the leafless garden and up the gravel path that led to the Cartwrights' back door. The light was on in the kitchen, and she could smell the warm oniony aroma of meat roasting in the oven. She took the key out of the zipper compartment in her purse and opened the kitchen door.

"It's five-thirty," said an unsmiling Kip who sat in the kitchen chair closest to the door. "I've been here for almost twenty minutes. Where have you been?"

The smile vanished from Missy's face as she closed the door behind her and entered the kitchen. "I was looking for my mitten," she said, shortly. "Sorry you had to wait."

Five

"ALL I want to know is where January went," Missy said to her mother as Mrs. Cartwright zipped her daughter into the red and white velvet formal she had gotten to wear at the Valentine's Day Dance that evening. "It seems like yesterday that Kip and I were off to the winter carnival, and now here it is time for the Valentine's Dance already." She fingered the golden locket engraved with her initials that hung around her neck. "Kippy gave me this last year for Valentine's Day—can it already be a whole year since we went to that dance?"

Her mother sighed and sat down on the bed. "You know what they say, darling—the older you get, the shorter the years and the longer the days. But I hardly think that you and Kip have reached that stage yet. Your father and I, on the other hand..." she said, laughing.

"Oh, Mother, how can you say that when Daddy came

home with those roses tonight? You two still act like lovebirds."

"Well—slightly older lovebirds," she conceded with a smile. "Although I must say that your father and I were a lot more affectionate in our carefree youth than are you and Kip. He's always so formal."

"Kip says P.D.A.'s are uncool," Missy answered, dabbing a bit of perfume behind each earlobe.

"P.D.A.?"

"Public Displays of Affection. Kip says that only the really uncool do more than hold hands in public."

"I suppose I agree with him to a certain extent," Mrs. Cartwright answered. "Displays of affection are private, but every now and then almost everybody likes a warm and cozy hug," she said, rising from the bed and putting her arms around her daughter, squeezing her tightly.

"Mom! You're going to mess up my dress," Missy complained, even though she herself returned the hug.

"Sorry, sorry!" she laughed, "I guess I got carried away. I don't think I did any permanent damage," she added, standing back and inspecting her daughter.

Missy examined herself in the mirror, pleased with her own reflection. She had wanted a red velvet dress this year, but all of the dresses the stores had were either velvet and the wrong color, or red, but not velvet. She and her mother had trooped in and out of every store in the Mall all day last Saturday, and the closest thing she could find was a wine-colored skirt and frilly white lace blouse. Her mother suggested that the sales-lady hold the outfit till Monday, in case they couldn't find anything else, and Missy and Mrs. Cartwright left the store, discouraged, but not desperate. Suddenly, out of the corner of her eye she saw a shop that she had never gone into before, one that mainly carried rather outlandish outfits in wild colors and outrageous designs. But there in the midst of silver lamé jumpsuits and magenta satin knickers was the most beautiful dress Missy had ever seen. Ankle-length with a high collar bordered by a white ruffle that stood up against her neck, with straight sleeves that were edged with the same ruffle that began inside the cuff, the fitted bodice flared out into a long graceful skirt that swirled when she moved. But it was the color that Missy loved the most—a rich, vibrant red, the color of the wild raspberries that she had picked as a child at her grandmother's house in Wisconsin. Raspberries and cream, she thought to herself when she looked at the dress hanging in the window. As Missy raced for the size six rack she found just one dress left in her size. Her heart beat wildly as she pulled off her clothes and eased the dress over her head; it was a perfect fit.

"Do you think my hair looks all right this way?" she asked her mother, inspecting the locks of braided hair on either side that she had caught in the back with a mother-of-pearl barrette. She took her brush and ran it through the rest of the hair that fell freely down her back and shone like a skein of golden thread.

"You look absolutely beautiful," her mother said, kissing her lightly on the cheek, careful not to muss the trace of powder blush that highlighted her daughter's high cheekbones.

The doorbell sounded and Missy cast her mother a panic-stricken look. "Kip's here! What did I do with my shoes?" she cried, searching for the silver, ankle-strapped evening slippers. Although she had worn them last year, they were practically brand new and matched her outfit perfectly.

"Underneath the dressing table," her mother said, pointing to the blue-flowered skirt of the white dressing table that matched the bedspread and curtains in Missy's room. "Here, you put on your shoes, Cinderella, and I'll tell the Prince to wait a moment."

"Oh, Kip will be all upset that I'm not ready yet," Missy groaned as she bent over to buckle her shoes. Flustered by the excitement and the pressure of knowing that Kip was waiting, Missy's fingers refused to work, and the strap of the shoe refused to go through the buckle. Missy suddenly felt boiling hot and close to tears. She plopped down on the dressing table chair and covered her face with her hands.

"Melissa?" her father called from the doorway. "Everything all right in here?"

"I can't get this shoe buckled, Daddy, and Kip's downstairs and we're going to be late, and now I'm getting a headache, and everything's going to be ruined because Kip will be mad at me and..."

"Hold on, hold on," her father said quietly, "you're getting yourself all in a dither. Just sit there and take a couple of deep breaths and relax—I'll fix your shoe."

Missy held out her foot and within seconds the shoe was buckled. She jumped up, ready to bound out of the room when her father put his hand on her shoulder. "Miss, this isn't like you, to fall apart because you can't get your shoe buckled. Is everything all right?"

"Everything's fine, Dad. I just wanted to be perfect, that's all, and there's always something going wrong."

Her father frowned a bit and shook his head. "Nobody's telling you to be perfect, Melissa."

"Well, I should be, that's all."

"Nobody's perfect, Miss—you shouldn't ask that of yourself. All you should want is to do your best—that's the most that can be expected of anyone."

"You sound just like Stephen," she mumbled.

"What?"

"I said you sound just like Stephen McRae. He's always telling me that I shouldn't be so hard on myself."

"He says that? Well, he's right—you should listen to what he says. I'm sure Kip would tell you the same thing."

Missy didn't answer as she checked herself in the mirror once again and dusted a bit of translucent powder over her nose. She turned toward her father and smiled. "I'm okay now, Dad. Thanks for helping me with my shoe."

"Anytime, kiddo, anytime," her father said as he kissed her on the cheek and watched her dash out of the room and down the stairs to meet Kip.

"How was the dance?" her mother asked as Missy came into the kitchen looking tired but happy, her shoes in her hand, the braids starting to work their way out of the mother-of-pearl barrette that was now angled rather crookedly in her hair.

"Amazing," she said, sitting down in a kitchen chair and closing her eyes. "Absolutely amazing. Did you see my corsage?" she asked, holding out her wrist to reveal a cluster of pink and red carnations entwined with white satin ribbon and green velvet leaves.

"Yes, I saw it when Kip came to pick you up. Would you like some cocoa or a cup of herb tea?" her mother asked.

"Mmm, some herb tea," she answered, getting up from her chair to get a cup.

"Stay there—I'll get the tea. I could use a cup myself," her mother said. "It's chilly in here—were you cold in that white wool jacket tonight?"

Missy shook her head. "No—everything was perfect: my dress, the flowers, my hair. Well, almost everything; Kip wondered why I had worn the same shoes I wore last year."

"I'm surprised—I thought he never noticed things like that."

"He didn't notice it until Poodie Hawkins brought it up, and then Kip got all upset that people were saying that I had worn old shoes to the dance."

"And what did you say?" Mrs. Cartwright asked, bringing Missy the tea and sitting down at the table across from her daughter.

"I said that they weren't old shoes and that Buffy was wearing the purse she always wore, and Tish had on the same taffeta plaid skirt she wore last year, so he calmed down."

"I think Kip Morgan has been given a bit too much spending money," Mrs. Cartwright said, frowning slightly. "Somebody should make him a little more aware of the price of things today."

"Are you kidding? Kip? His dad is made of money," Missy exclaimed.

"Yes," her mother continued, "but Kip's father earned that money by working hard day and night to build a successful business. If you've earned money honestly, then who's to say how you ought to spend it? But until Kip goes out and starts earning his own fortune, he should be a bit more conservative about

how he advises other people to spend their money."
Mrs. Cartwright took a sip of her tea. "Sorry to go
off on a tirade," she added, "but I just had to say all
that. Now, tell me about the dance."

"It was—glorious!" Missy sighed. "The gym was all
decorated with the hearts and cupids we made last
weekend. Tish and Jimbo and some of the seniors hung
them this afternoon. Kip and I would have helped dec-
orate, but he had a tennis clinic after school and I
wanted to get home and wash my hair for tonight. Anyway, they hung those and streamers of pink, white, and
red crepe paper, and put lacy doilies and ribbons everywhere. The senior and junior class treasuries pooled
their money and bought big bunches of red and pink
and white carnations which were just all over the
place—on the punch table, on little stands near the
entrance—everywhere! And Mrs. Mitchell and some
lady from a catering service in town did a terrific job
with the food. There was this red punch with an ice
heart decorated with maraschino cherries floating in
the punch bowl, and a pink and white cake all decorated
with hearts, and bowls of red and white candies, and
long, slender red and white candles burning everywhere. At the last dance they turned down the lights
and all you could see were the flickering candles in the
darkness. The spicy clove scent of the carnations filled
the room, and the music was soft—it was fantastic!"

"Did you and Kip dance a lot?"

"Every dance," Missy said, yawning. "I got sort of
tired, but Kip said it was important for us to be seen
dancing all the time so that people would know what
a tight couple we are."

Mrs. Cartwright looked at Missy a bit strangely and

opened her mouth to speak. But instead, she bit her lip and took another sip of her tea.

"Kip's funny sometimes," Missy continued. "Buffy was telling me this crazy story about this crazy girl in her gym class who studies modern dance and makes up all these wild dances, and it was a really funny story the way Buffy was telling it. Anyway, we both started giggling, and Kip and Tink turned around to see what was going on. So all of a sudden Kip tells me to put down my punch and leads me off onto the dance floor. I asked him what was going on, and he said that I was making a spectacle of myself, laughing like that, and that he had to keep an eye on me every minute because all eyes were on us at the dance."

"You shouldn't let him talk to you like that," Mrs. Cartwright said, shaking her head. "It's normal for you to want to laugh at a party. You're young—you ought to be able to relax and have fun, not constantly be worrying about how you look to the other people in the room."

"I guess," Missy mused, "but he's right in a way. People expect us always to do the right thing."

"Yes, you can do the right thing, but it shouldn't prevent you from having a relaxed, happy time at a dance."

"Now you're starting to sound like Stephen," Missy muttered.

"Stephen! Oh, I'm so glad you reminded me," her mother said, getting up from the table and going over to the refrigerator.

"Reminded you of what?"

"Of this," her mother said, taking something out of the refrigerator wrapped in waxed paper. "Here, Stephen McRae brought these over for you at about nine o'clock tonight. He said that he knew that you were at the dance but that he wanted you to find these when you got home." Mrs. Cartwright handed the gift to Missy and stretched her arms over her own head, yawning. "Look, Missouri, I'm going to bed. Turn off the lights before you go upstairs, hmm?" her mother said, kissing Missy on the top of her head as she walked out of the kitchen. "I'm glad you had a good time tonight," she called back over her shoulder.

"Thanks, Mom—'night," Missy called back as she peeled back the layers of waxed paper to find out what Stephen's gift was.

"Oh," she murmured as she saw what was inside: a bouquet of deep purple violets, surrounded by a circlet of pink and red rosebuds all held together by a lacy white doily and a pink satin ribbon. Attached to the bow was a small white card. Missy opened the card and read the message inside, written in Stephen's own handwriting: For Melissa, Who Is Always Special, But Especially So On Valentine's Day. From your admirer, Stephen.

Missy just sat there for a while in the darkened kitchen, the delicate scent of violets filling the air. "For Melissa who is always special," she repeated out loud to herself, her voice echoing in the quiet night kitchen.

A fleeting image of Stephen, his bright eyes flashing with energy, bringing the bouquet to her house when he knew she was off at the dance made her eyes brim over with tears.

She rose from her chair, still dressed in her velvet dress, Kip's corsage wilting on her wrist, and got a small crystal vase from the top shelf over the sink. Carrying the vase, the bouquet of violets, and her shoes, Missy turned out the lights downstairs and headed up to her bedroom, dropping off her shoes before she entered the bathroom to fill the vase from the tap.

Careful not to spill any of the water, she brought the vase back to her bedroom and set it down on the night table next to her bed. She put the bouquet in the vase and stood back to look at it. In the soft light of her bedroom, next to the white wicker headboard and against the blue and white wallpaper with its tiny sprigs of forget-me-nots, the violet bouquet looked like an heirloom photo magically come to life at the stroke of midnight. An old-fashioned sweetness of rose and violet scented the room and filled Missy with a happy ease, a light bubbly feeling that took away her earlier weariness. A dreamy sleep began to overtake her, and she struggled to get out of her uncomfortable clothes and into the downy softness of her blue flannel nightgown. As she folded back the bedspread and climbed into bed, a whiff of violet greeted her once again.

"Stephen," she said as she lay down in bed and snuggled under the covers. "Stephen, who thinks I'm always special," she whispered as she drifted off to sleep.

Six

MISSY PICKED up the phone and dialed the number that was written in her parents' phone book. The phone rang three times before a voice answered.

"Hello?"

"Hello, Stephen?"

"Yes?"

"This is Missy."

There was silence on the phone. Then Stephen cleared his throat and began again to speak, trying to sound as casual as he could, knowing why she was calling. "Oh, hello, Melissa. How're ya doing?"

"Fine, Stephen. Uhm, I called to thank you for the lovely flowers you brought over last night. It was the prettiest bouquet I've ever gotten. Nobody ever gave me violets before."

Stephen laughed with pleasure. "You see, they don't grow flowers in 'Melissa blue'—well, I guess cornflow-ers are that color, but somehow bringing a girl a bouquet of cornflowers just doesn't have the same ring as bring a bouquet of violets."

"And not just violets—rosebuds too! It really was awfully sweet of you to do that. And the note, well, the note was the best part of all."

"I meant it, Melissa. I wouldn't have written that unless I meant it."

"That's why I liked it the best," Missy told him. "Most people just write a bunch of soppy stuff whether they mean it or not."

"Well, I don't, ever," Stephen declared. "Uhhm, I know that you're always pretty busy," he began hesitantly, but uhh... I'm having some people I've met at *Wordsmith* over to my house tonight. They're all in the orchestra, too, and we thought we'd just get together and play some music and sit around....if you're not busy, do you think you could come?"

Missy waited a few seconds before answering. She really wasn't all that busy tonight; after last night's dance nobody really felt like going anywhere. She had told Buffy that she and Kip might come over and watch the video cassette if Buffy's father had brought home something good, but that wasn't really definite. How could she say no to a simple thing like dropping over to Stephen's house after he had brought her the violets? "What time are your friends supposed to come over?" she asked tentatively.

"About 7:30. Can you come?" Stephen asked rather anxiously.

"Sure," Missy said, "sure I can come."

"Super!" Stephen shouted in her ear. "Okay, see you tonight, Melissa."

"Right, Stephen," she said, "'bye."

As she hung up the phone she realized exactly what she had done. All of Stephen's friends would know who she was. How could she keep this a secret from Kip and The Group? They would never understand why she hadn't simply said no to Stephen's offer.

"Something wrong, Miss?" her mother asked as she came into the kitchen and found Missy just staring at the floor, standing next to the telephone.

"No, not really. Stephen McRae just invited me to a party at his house tonight and I said I would come."

"Funny, that doesn't sound like a problem to me," her mother said.

"It isn't really—it's just I don't know what to tell Kip and the others about where I was tonight when they ask me why I wasn't with them."

"Oh, I see. They don't get along with Stephen and his friends?"

"No, not at all."

"Just tell Kip the truth, honey—that's always the best thing to do," Mrs. Cartwright told her, but Missy was not quite convinced.

"Kip just won't understand," she mumbled as she went up to her bedroom to decide what would be the right thing to wear for people who wrote for literary magazines and played musical instruments.

As Missy went up the path to the McRae house, she could hear voices coming from the living room, and the sound of a piano. I wonder if I'm wearing the right clothes, she thought to herself, nervous at the idea of entering a roomful of people alone without Kip to lead the way. She tugged at the grosgrain ribbon in her hair. Maybe she should have worn her hair with the little braids at the sides gathered back in barrettes; maybe that would have looked more "artsy." Oh, well, it was too late now, she told herself. She had decided on her navy blue corduroy pants, a light blue oxford cloth shirt with a navy blue monogram of her initials, and a navy blazer—that was always a safe choice. Still, her nerves were getting the best of her.

As soon as she rang the bell she heard footsteps approaching, and within seconds Stephen had opened the door and was showing her inside.

"Melissa, terrific!" Stephen said, greeting her warmly. "I was hoping that you hadn't changed your mind. Come on in—everybody else is here."

Missy walked into the living room and into a sea of slightly familiar faces whose names she did not know. From the moment she walked in, however, she knew that she had chosen the wrong clothes for the evening.

"Here, sit down over here on the couch," Stephen said, threading her through the group on the floor and over to the couch. "Everybody, this is Melissa Anne Cartwright. And this," he said, pointing to the people on the floor and sitting next to Missy on the couch, "is Holly Block, Noel Eliot, Andrew Pearl, Barbara Francis, Dylan Hunt, and Caitlin Erinns."

"Hi," they all chorused as Stephen introduced them, and Missy braved a smile and a timid "hi" in return as she sat down on the edge of the couch.

"Would you like some hot cider or jasmine tea?" Stephen asked her.

"Cider, thank you," she answered, having no idea what jasmine tea was. Stephen quickly returned with a rough pottery mug of hot cider garnished with a cinnamon stick, and handed it to Missy, who was glad to have something to do with her hands. Never before had she felt so uncomfortable or out of place. And never before had she seen people at a party dressed in such a wild assortment of outfits. Sitting near Missy on the floor was the girl Stephen had pointed out as Holly Block, whom Missy knew to be the poetry editor of *Wordsmith*. Holly's waist-length black hair was caught back in an oriental bamboo barrette woven to look like a butterfly, and large golden pierced-earring hoops hung from her ears. Her black kimono top, with its long, flowing sleeves and brightly colored floral pattern, hung gracefully over her blue-jean skirt and black suede boots, and Indian bangle bracelets made of colored glass jangled on her wrists. Noel Eliot, the boy sitting next to Holly, was a senior, Missy knew, for she had read in the school paper that he had won an early acceptance and scholarship to an eastern college—but Missy couldn't remember which one. He had the beginnings of a blond beard growing on his chin, and was wearing a long-sleeved tee shirt with the words "DON'T READ THIS" silk-screened on it in red ink. Another boy was wearing an embroidered peasant shirt, a girl was decked out in an African print caftan, and one girl had on the magenta knickers and blouse that Missy had seen in the shop where she had bought her Valentine's Dance dress. Missy sat there, perched on the couch, taking tiny sips from the mug to make the cider last as long as possible, wishing she had never decided to come.

"Are we going to sit here yakking all night or did we come here to play?" the girl in the caftan asked Stephen, who started to laugh.

"Okay, you're right, Barbara—let's play," Stephen

said, opening the hall closet and taking out a black case while Holly and some of the others went off into the den.

Play what? Stephen hadn't mentioned any games when he told Missy about the party. What did people like this play, anyway? Backgammon? Scrabble? Charades? Oh, terrific, Missy thought to herself. I've risked a fight with Kip and The Group to watch a bunch of people in weird outfits play Scrabble.

But suddenly the people who had gone into the den began returning, bringing with them metal folding stands, black and brown cases of assorted sizes, and straight-backed chairs. Only Missy had remained in her seat.

"Set up over here near the piano so that I don't have to play way out in left field," Holly told them as she shuffled through a sheaf of sheet music and opened the keyboard of the McRae's baby grand piano. "Nothing like playing in the house of a piano teacher," she called to Stephen. "I never worry about the piano being out of tune here—your mom must have this thing tuned every couple of weeks."

"Not quite," Stephen said, laughing, "but their piano tuner is this crazy guy with a long beard who meditates and belongs to a Zen Buddhist temple, so I think my mom calls him a lot just because she likes talking to him. Also, he used to be a pastry chef and everytime he comes over here he brings some fancy cake that he and his wife baked."

"Oh—I know that guy," called Barbara Francis, who was taking a flute out of its case and putting it together, from her seat near the couch. "His wife is a singer with a couple of the Renaissance music groups I play with."

"Yeah, that's him," Stephen said, taking the clarinet reed out of the case and putting it in his mouth to moisten it before he began to play.

The others all took out various musical instruments—a slim, black oboe which made an almost Oriental sound when Noel put it to his lips and began to play, and a golden French horn that sounded faraway and soft when Dylan Hunt muffled its notes by putting his hand inside the bell-shaped opening where the sound came out. Huge piles of sheet music began to litter the music stands as they all took their places before the stands and started tuning up.

This is another world, Missy thought to herself, feeling more uncomfortable than she had ever felt in her life. A world of Buddhist piano tuners who baked cakes, of composers whose names she did not recognize, of orchestras and small chamber music groups—a whole new society that was as foreign to her as a remote tribe on a South Seas isle.

Missy looked down at her lap and played with a frayed thread on the buttonhole of her jacket. Why had Stephen invited her? Was this his way of getting back for the incident at lunch? Had he brought her here, among his friends, so that she would feel totally out of place, unwanted, and ignored? Yes, that must be it, Missy decided. She should not have come. Stick with your own kind, Kip always told her, and it looked as though, once again, Kip knew best.

A hand on her shoulder startled her, and she looked up to find Stephen standing next to her, the clarinet reed still sticking out of his mouth like an overgrown toothpick. "Things get a bit hectic around here right

before we start playing. Can you read music?" he asked
her, smiling warmly.

Missy shook her head. Another closed world.

"Well, then I won't tell you to come over and sit
where you can see the music. I think if you stay where
you are you can hear the group the best. I've got to
warn you, we're not exactly ready for Carnegie Hall."

Carnegie Hall, Missy thought. That's that great big
concert hall in New York where everybody dreams of
playing one day. Ha ha, she laughed to herself, see,
I do know something about music after all.

"Can I get you some more cider before we start?"
Stephen asked.

"No, I'm just fine," Missy answered, determined not
to let him know how out of place she really felt. She
was the queen of the winter carnival, an honors student, *and* Kip Morgan's girlfriend, and she wasn't going
to let a bunch of weirdos make *her* feel like a reject.

"Okay," he said, walking back to his chair, "prepare
yourself, Melissa."

Someone suggested a piece with which they could
begin, and they all turned to their sheet music and
found their copies of that particular quintet.

"We're not actually a quintet, 'cause we've got an
extra member—Holly, playing the piano," Stephen
called to her.

"Yeah, they tried to get rid of me, but I held my
ground," Holly teased.

Well, Missy thought, I'm just going to hold my
ground, too. She shifted positions on the sofa and sat
up straight, looking Stephen directly in the eye.

He winked at her, and Missy smiled in spite of herself.

Suddenly the room became very quiet, and everyone looked at Noel Eliot, who was tapping a rhythm with his toe.

"One, two, three," he said softly, the oboe poised in front of his lips.

As if by magic the silence was broken by a wonderful sound. Like a wind off the lake, the music swept the room with a clear, bright harmony, sometimes quick, sometimes slowing to a moody, almost haunting sadness. Missy closed her eyes and let the music flow over her, just as it had under the starlit summer skies when she had heard the symphony at Ravinia Park as a child. A peaceful calm overtook her, filling her with a happy lightness. When the music ended, she opened her eyes.

"That was wonderful!" she exclaimed, before she even realized that she was speaking.

"Oh dear, at last—a fan!" Caitlin Erinns giggled. "Stephen, why didn't you bring her around before? More, more, come on Melissa—we need all the praise we can get!"

Missy laughed and applauded, breaking up the whole group, who stood before their chairs and bowed.

"Take all you can get," Holly muttered, "I don't know how long we can fool Melissa into thinking that we actually know what we're doing."

They sat down again, turned to another piece of music and began to play once more. They continued playing for almost an hour; each piece new and different, unexpected, fresh. Every now and then someone goofed, and the group moaned and groaned, teasing the person who had botched it, starting over to correct the mistake. But even with the various slip-ups the music was beautiful, made even more exciting because the

players were actually there, right before Missy. Al
though she enjoyed listening with her eyes closed, let
ting her mind wander, floating free, she found it eve
better to keep them open so she could watch what wa
going on around her. How hard they all worked, cor
centrating on getting the notes right, trying to sta
together and work as a team. Just like a crack footba
squad, Missy thought; each one taking his or her ow
part, playing it as well as possible, yet never forgettin
that it was the group effort that really counted. Sh
watched Stephen's face as he played the clarinet par
raising his eyebrows when he had to reach a high note
playing with his chin nearly touching his chest whe
he tried for a low sound. They're all in their own worl
now, Missy thought, conscious only of the music, of th
sound that they are making together. A strange feelin
began to creep over her that increased the longer th
music was played. A good world, the voice in her hea
told her, and by being here you're a part of it, too.

"Are you guys ready for a break?" Mrs. McRae aske
coming in from the kitchen when she heard the mus
stop after one particularly long piece.

"Oh, are we!" Holly moaned, resting her head on th
top of the piano.

"I'm wasted," Dylan mumbled, his mouth all re
from where the mouthpiece of the French horn ha
been.

"Well, come on, then, somebody help me bring th
goodies in here," Mrs. McRae called over her should
as she disappeared into the kitchen.

"Coming," Stephen shouted as he put down his cla
inet and stood up, stretching.

"Can I help?" Missy asked, hesitantly.

The Preppy Problem 75

"Yeah, you can be our groupie and official munchie-carrier," Noel said, laughing, popping her on the head lightly with his hand. "I hereby appoint you to the Munchie Patrol."

Missy laughed and followed the group into the kitchen where Mrs. McRae had set out plates of sandwiches, cans of soda and a pitcher of orange juice, and a tray of cupcakes.

"A feast!" Andrew Pearl said, breaking the ring off a can of root beer and drinking half the can in one long gulp. "Bassooning makes me thirsty," he explained to Holly who was shaking her head in amazement as he took another swig and emptied the can.

They all carried the food and drinks back into the living room where they set it down on the coffee table, filled up paper plates, and sat down wherever there was room.

"Mom, is there any mayo?" Stephen shouted as he bit into his ham sandwich.

"There is—if you want it come and get it," his mother answered from the kitchen.

"I'll go," Missy said, beginning to get up from the couch.

"No you won't," Holly said, taking her arm and preventing her from moving. "No serving of the men here. If he wants the mayo enough, he'll find the strength to get it for himself," Holly said, laughing.

"I'm going to cancel your subscription to *MS*," Stephen threatened playfully as he got up from the floor. "Is there anything I can get you while I'm up doing things equally?"

"Uh huh," Holly said, smiling. "A little more mustard, please," she told him, handing him her sandwich on its plate.

"I let you get away with murder," Stephen muttered as he walked off into the kitchen. He returned a moment later with the sandwiches and two jars—one of mayonnaise and one of mustard. "I brought the works just in case," he said slathering his sandwich. "Anybody else?"

"I'd like a little mustard," Missy said, reaching for the knife.

"Oh, no, allow me," he offered, shooting a look at Holly and spreading mustard on Missy's sandwich.

"See," Holly whispered loudly enough for Stephen to hear, "you've got to train them right while they're young."

Missy laughed in amazement. She had never seen a girl act like that around a boy—so strong and at the same time with a sense of humor that softened the strength.

"That's enough out of you," Noel said from his seat on one of the folding chairs. "Boy, sometimes I wonder with all the girls out there, why I had to team up with the Gloria Steinem of Highland Park High."

"Because you loooooove me," Holly sang out, making everyone laugh, including Noel. "He's really crazy about me—he just doesn't know it yet," Holly whispered to Missy.

"I heard that," Noel said. "I don't know about being crazy *about* you, but after being with you for a few hours I certainly feel crazy."

"Love, pure and simple," Holly said, taking another bite of her sandwich. "You know what Billy Boy said

Love is blind and lovers cannot see/ The pretty follies that themselves commit.'"

"Oh, no, there she goes quoting Shakespeare again," Noel groaned, putting his hands up over his face. "And do you always have to refer to him as 'Billy Boy'?"

"Okay, 'Willie Boy,' then, is that better?" she answered him.

"Hopeless," Noel said, looking at Missy. "Absolutely hopeless. I'll bet Melissa doesn't go around boring people silly with Shakespeare."

"I don't know about that," Holly answered him. "Last year we were in the same Honors English class, and Melissa gave a really good oral report on *Romeo and Juliet*."

Missy looked at Holly, surprised. "How do you remember that? That was almost a year ago!"

"Oh, I remember almost everything. I've got one of those photographic memories. You probably wouldn't remember me, though. I was much shyer last year. I sat in the back near the bulletin boards and never opened my mouth."

Missy tried to picture the sophomore English classroom, but all she could remember was a quiet, rather overweight girl who wore wire-rimmed glasses and sat in the back. Suddenly she realized that the girl she was thinking of was Holly. "But you..." Missy began, not knowing quite how to phrase her question.

"The fat girl in the back with the glasses. Yup, that was me." Holly grimaced. See what six months of yogurt and chicken and a pair of contact lenses can do?"

"Now if they could only do something about her mouth," Noel groaned.

"All part of the new me," Holly chattered. "Now that

I've gone the glamor route they can't shut me up," she giggled, holding the flowered sleeve of her kimono in front of her face like a veil. She took her arm down and faced Missy again. "You really write well," she told her, "you ought to submit something to *Wordsmith*. Do you like poetry?"

"I don't know," Missy said, munching her sandwich and leaning back on the couch. "I mean, I like the poetry units in class, but I never thought about it much once class was over."

"e.e. cummings—that's who I like," Dylan announced. "It takes you an hour to figure out how to read the poems, with all those small letters and words running together and no punctuation, but once you get it—he's something else."

"Yeah, or A.E. Housman—I cried the first time I read that poem about the young athlete who died," Caitlin confided.

"Oh, so did I," Holly agreed.

"You'd cry over a cat food commercial," Noel teased. "Boy, have you ever gone to a movie with this one? You have to bring a tarpaulin if you want to sit next to her and not get soaked. When we went to that Humphrey Bogart festival at the 'Biograph' in Chicago I practically drowned during *Casablanca*."

"Go on, you were just as upset as I was," Holly teased back. "He tries to pretend he's unaffected, but suddenly I'll hear this really loud hiccup, and I'll know that the movie is getting to him."

"I hiccup, wise guy, because of the popcorn," Noel defended.

"Sure, that's what they all say," Holly answered.

nodding her head. "Do you ever go to the 'Biograph', Missy?"

"No, I'm not even sure where it is," Missy answered truthfully.

"Stephen, she should come with us the next time we go into Chicago," Holly suggested. "We all load into somebody's car and drive into the city and have dinner at this great vegetarian Indian restaurant. They have these terrific vegetable curries and all the waitresses wear saris—you know, those long, flowing scarf-like dresses that Indian women wear. Some of the women even have red dots on their foreheads for decoration, and pierced noses. One of them has a ruby right on the side of her nostril, here," she told Missy, pointing to the side of her nose.

"Get to the point," Stephen laughed, hitting her lightly on her arm.

"Oh, yeah. Well, after dinner we walk down the street to the 'Biograph' on Lincoln Avenue—that's near Old Town, where all the artsy shops and little boutiques with Indian bedspreads and earrings and incense..."

"I know where Old Town is," Missy explained quickly. "I went there with my mother once. She took me to an antique shop, and then we had lunch at an old-fashioned ice cream parlor."

"That's right—well the 'Biograph' isn't too far from that part of town. They show all these old movies there, and when there's a Bogart festival or an Ingrid Bergman week, or even *The Rocky Horror Picture Show* we all go together and make an adventure out of it. Next time we go you'll have to come along."

"That sounds great," Missy answered. "I've never tasted Indian food."

"Spicy, spicy, spicy," said Andrew. "It's the best."

"And they play Indian records, you know, sitar music like Ravi Shankar plays," Holly explained.

"Speaking of music, it's getting kind of late. I think we'd better play one more piece before we call it a night, and if we don't play it soon, I'll be too tired to read the notes," Stephen yawned.

"Yeah, one more piece," Holly said, moving over to the piano.

"Oh, I think I ate too much," Dylan moaned as he picked up his French horn. "You know what happened the last time I ate a bunch of stuff before we played."

"Do we have to hear about your barfing episodes again?" Barbara said in mock disgust, looking at Missy and shaking her head. "What Dylan has in talent he lacks in manners," she whispered. "Boy, are you being treated to the nitty-gritty of the *Wordsmith* staff."

"What you see is what you get," Dylan said as he raised his French horn to his lips and looked over toward Noel who would give them the signal to play.

As the music started again Missy leaned back on the soft couch cushions, slipped off her shoes and tucked her feet up under her. She tried to listen for each of the individual instruments—the clarinet line, then the oboe, then the flute, but unless there was a solo part featuring one of the instruments, it was almost impossible to pick any one out. A real team, she thought to herself again. A real team.

"I'm going to go home and flop into bed," Caitlin Erinns groaned after they finished their last piece and began to pack up their instruments.

"Me too," Andrew agreed, "and I have hockey practice tomorrow morning. I'm never going to make it."

"You play hockey?" Missy asked, surprised that someone who played the bassoon would also play hockey.

"Yeah, I figure it this way. If I don't make it into the Chicago Symphony, I can always join the Blackhawks."

"Right, Pearl," Holly chortled, "dream on."

"You'll see," he answered, "this kid is a class act."

"You're all class acts," Mrs. McRae said, coming in to the living room, "but could you get your class act together and clean up some of this mess? Stephen, fold up the chairs and put them back in the den closet. I've got a new pupil coming for a piano lesson tomorrow and I don't want her mother to think I give wild Saturday night parties. Could somebody take the empty soda pop cans into the kitchen?"

"Sure," Holly said, bending down to help pick up the litter on the coffee table.

Finally everything was in relatively good shape, the music stands and chairs folded away and the crumbs swept up.

"I'll walk you home," Stephen told Missy as he handed her coat to her. "It's too late for you to walk around by yourself."

"Okay," Missy agreed, and put on her coat, saying goodnight to Dylan and Caitlin who were heading out the door.

Bundled up in their heavy coats, the rest of the crowd called to Mrs. McRae to say thanks, and went outside.

"I'll take everybody home," Noel said, pointing to his father's station wagon, which was parked at the curb. "Where do you live, Melissa?"

"She just lives down the block and over a street," Stephen told him. "I'll walk her home."

"All right," Noel agreed. "Glad you could come, Melissa."

"Yeah," Holly added, "and the next time we trek down to the Biograph, you'll have to come with us."

"Super," Missy answered, "I'd love that."

"Goodnight," Stephen called as the others piled into the station wagon and he and Missy hurried down the street, freezing in the winter night air.

Mrs. Cartwright had left the light on in the kitchen for Missy, and she quickly found her keys in her purse.

"It's really late, so I'm just going to head back to my house," Stephen said as she opened the door.

"Yes, it is late," Missy agreed, looking at the clock near the door, which said almost midnight. "I'm supposed to be in by twelve—and that's only on special occasions. Usually it's 10:30."

"Then you'd better go in," Stephen said, his breath white with the cold.

"Okay," she answered, looking down at the snow. "I had a wonderful time tonight, Stephen. Your friends are great, and the music was even better."

"They liked you too," he said, "especially when you applauded."

"I had to applaud—you deserved it."

Stephen was quiet for a moment before he spoke again, looking directly into Missy's eyes. "I'm really glad you could come," he said softly.

"I'm glad you asked me," she answered, meeting his eyes with her own.

"Goodnight, Melissa," he replied, taking one step down the stairs.

"Goodnight, Stephen," she said without moving.

He turned to go down the next step and begin his walk back home when he hesitated for a moment, stepped up to the top step again, and whirled around, kissing Missy lightly on her lips.

"'Night," he whispered before he dashed down the steps and began racing home in the cold darkness.

Missy stood on the step for a moment, a chill running down her back. She took in a deep breath of the February wind and held it, hoping that it would clear her head of the troubling but at the same time wonderful thought that was echoing in her mind.

"Stephen kissed me," she finally said out loud, exhaling the air in a gust. No, it wasn't really a kiss, she told herself. Not really.

Stephen kissed me and I'm glad, her mind's voice insisted.

Stephen kissed me and I'm glad—I think, she decided as she entered the house, shivering with cold.

A piece of paper was lying on the kitchen table, held down by an apple that her mother had left out for her.

Missy walked over to the table, picked up the apple, and looked at the note.

"Kip called," the message read.

Seven

"WHERE WERE you last night?" Buffy questioned as she came upstairs into Missy's room. "Kip tried to call you from my house, but your Dad said that you had gone someplace. Where'd you go?"

Missy continued making her bed, folding the blue and white striped top sheet over the light blue down quilt. "I had to go to this thing," she stalled.

"What 'thing'? I thought you were going to watch the video with us—everybody came, you know."

"Well, I wanted to come, but my mom made me go to this thing, so I couldn't."

"What THING for goodness' sake!" Buffy demanded, walking around to the head of the bed so that Missy could no longer avoid her eyes.

"This, uhh, little party that my...my cousin Marcia was giving."

"Your cousin Marcia? You haven't seen her in years.

Why did she suddenly invite you to a party? What kind of party anyway?" Buffy asked her suspiciously.

"A...birthday party. Yes, a birthday party. See, she was just fifteen and she doesn't have a whole lot of friends, so she asked me to come so there would be more people."

"So how come you didn't ask Kip?"

"There...weren't going to be enough girls, so she told me to come alone," Missy lied, getting herself in deeper and deeper.

"First party I've ever heard of where there were too many girls," Buffy said, shaking her head. "Was it a good party at least?"

"No, I had a terrible time. I wanted to get home early enough to come over to your house, but by the time my uncle Ernie drove me home it was after eleven and too late to call. I sure was mad. I told my mom that that's the last time she ever makes me do anything like that again," Missy said, beginning to believe her own fib.

"Well, Kip was even more ticked off than that. Boy, you should have heard him when he was trying to get you and the phone was busy, and then he finally got through to find out that you weren't even there. He was so mad I thought he was going to burst a blood vessel!"

Missy flushed slightly, worried already about the inevitable confrontation. The last thing Kip ever wanted was to lose his cool in front of his friends, and now she was the cause of his making a scene. "No wonder he hasn't called yet today," Missy said, pulling the bedspread up over the pillow and making a crease between the pillow's rise and the flat blankets.

"He'll call in a little while," Buffy answered. "He

and Tink decided to play some racquetball this morning, and they went over to the club at about 10:00. Tink called me right as they were leaving. They were taking Kip's car and said that I should meet them here. We were thinking about going into town to Startay's to look at the new Rod Stewart album and then going over to Lou's for a hamburger. Sound okay?"

"Sure, sounds fine," Missy answered. "I have some French homework, but I can do that later."

"You worry about your homework too much," Buffy told her. "You like my nail polish?" She held up her hands to reveal perfectly filed, almond-shaped nails painted with a light peach-colored polish. "I got it at Fields' yesterday—Poodie came with me. She got some called 'Candyspun Pink,' but I liked this 'Peach Blossom' better. More classic."

"Great," Missy told her without really looking. "I need some new nail polish, too, but I haven't had time to buy any."

"No, you've been too busy helping out poor, nurdy Cousin Marcia and ignoring your own life. Say, I've got an idea—why don't we head into town now and go to Clark's Drugstore? I can get that new lip gloss I've been wanting, and we can pick out some nail polish for you. We'll tell your mom that when the guys call she should tell them to meet us at Clark's. How 'bout it?"

"Sure," Missy said without enthusiasm. "Sure, we can go to Clark's."

They went downstairs to get their coats from the closet and began layering on their heavy clothing.

"Are you feeling okay?" Buffy asked as Missy bent down to pull on her boots.

"I'm fine," Missy answered. "Why?"

"You're just acting kind of quiet," Buffy said. "You're not mad about something, are you?"

Missy stood up and looked at Buffy. "Don't be crazy, Buff—why should I be mad at you?"

"You never know. One minute you're friends with somebody, and the next minute she's saying all sorts of things about you behind your back."

Missy shook her head. "You ought to know me better than that. I'd never do anything like that. Who acts that way?"

Buffy was quiet for a minute. "I probably shouldn't say anything."

"What?"

"It's just that, well, Poodie asked me if there was something wrong between you and Kip."

Missy flushed. "When did she ask that?"

Buffy ran her hand through her chin-length auburn hair. "Yesterday, when we were having lunch at Lou's. She said that at the Valentine's Dance Kip seemed a little upset with you."

"Oh, she must have meant when we were laughing about that girl in your gym class who does the modern dances," Missy said, mimicking Buffy's imitation of the girl's wild dances.

"No, not about that."

"About what, then?" Missy asked as she pulled her purse over her shoulder and yelled upstairs to her mother about the message that she should give to the boys when they called.

"About your shoes," Buffy told her as they walked down the back steps and into the alley to take the shortcut to the main street where they could watch for a public bus.

"Oh, that—well, what did Poodie bring my shoes up for in the first place? Kip never notices things like shoes, but if Poodie makes a point of saying that they're a year old, you can't expect Kip not to notice." Missy said angrily.

"Well, that's not all Poodie said," Buffy continued.

"What else did she say?" Missy asked, stopping in the middle of the road, her hands on her hips.

"She said that you've started acting less cool than you used to and that you'd better watch it or else Kip is going to find a new girl for a steady," Buffy reported, her eyes growing wide, waiting for Missy's reaction.

"Why doesn't Poodie mind her own business?" Missy said, starting to walk again. "What does she have to start stirring up trouble for?"

"Beats me," Buffy told her as they waited for the bus that was heading their way.

"I think it's that she and Win aren't getting along too well and that rather than deal with her own problems she's mixing in other people's business," Missy said as they boarded the bus and took their seats.

"Maybe you're right," Buffy said, looking out the window. "But why didn't you get new shoes for the dance? I mean, I wore my last year's purse, but then, I'm not Kip Morgan's girl."

"What's that supposed to mean?"

"Nothing, except that if you're going with the most popular boy in school, you'd better protect your position. There are an awful lot of girls who would be more than willing to replace you."

"Like Poodie, you mean?"

"No, I think she's pretty tight with Win, even if they're having problems right now. But there are oth-

ers—juniors, sophomores, freshmen, even seniors—
who would be more than happy to be crowned queen
of dances and things."

"Well, what makes you think that it's all Kip?" Missy
asked indignantly.

Buffy just looked at Missy, startled. "I mean...I'm
not saying that you're not pretty or anything but..."

"But it's Kip who brings in the votes, I know," Missy
said, slumping down in her seat. "I know it's Kip. I was
never queen of anything before I met him." She looked
out the window for a moment before turning back to
Buffy. "But then, he was never king of anything either."

"That's because he was too young to run," Buffy said
defensively.

"I suppose," Missy reluctantly agreed.

"Look, Missy, I wouldn't dream of telling you what
to do, but all I'm saying is that maybe for the next few
weeks or so you'd better devote all your attention to
Kip, just in case," Buffy said, getting up from her seat
as their stop came up.

"Maybe," Missy said slowly, "maybe."

They got off the bus and entered Clark's, heading
straight for the cosmetics counter.

"Look, Miss," Buffy said excitedly, "They've already
got the new spring colors in!" She smeared a streak of
bright green eyeshadow on the back of her hand.
"Ooh—'African Emerald,'" she cried, showing Missy
the colored line on her hand.

"Yes! And this one here is 'Tasmania Taupe.' What
weird names these things have. 'Southern Hemisphere
Hues'—oh, I see. All the colors are named for some

place south of the equator. I love this 'New Zealand Teal,' don't you?" Missy said.

"Yeah, but if I wanted a geography lesson, I'd buy a book. I'll stick to 'Kiss Me Kream' and 'Boom Boom Bronze!' Look, how do you think this goes with my coloring?"

"Don't use it on your face," Missy warned her. "My mom says that you should only test these things on your hand."

"Oh, well, too late now. If I get leprosy, I'll send you a letter from the leper colony. How do my eyes look?" Buffy asked, batting the lashes of her huge, light brown eyes.

"Nice, but I like that lavender stuff you usually use better than all that brown," Missy said, her hand striped with four different blue eyeshadows and two rosy blush-ons.

"Let's get you some nail polish," Buffy said, moving down the counter to the nail polish display. She turned the rotating stand around and around to examine all of the latest colors. "What do you like the best—frosted or creme?"

"I don't know," Missy said, coming over to join her. "What do you think?"

"This," Buffy announced, taking a bottle of "Sunrise Coral" from the rack. "But wait, here are the guys— let's ask them."

"Hi!" Missy said brightly as Kip and Tink approached, their duffel bags and racquets in their hands. "Who won?"

"Who do you think?" Kip asked her as he walked up beside her and put his arm around her shoulder.

"You," she said, looking up into his cool, gray eyes, and smiling.

"Of course," Kip answered. "Where were you last night?"

"She had to go to her nurdy cousin's party to give the thing some class," Buffy said as she showed Tink the two eyeshadow colors she planned to buy.

"What cousin? How come you didn't tell me?" Kip asked, looking down at her, his arm still around her shoulder.

"Uhh...because my mother sprang the whole thing on me only yesterday," Missy lied once again.

"Yeah, and there weren't enough girls, so she had to go alone," Buffy said as she examined the effect of the eyeshadows on her eyes in the mirror above the display case.

"You still should have let me know. I don't like to be left in the dark about where you are," Kip said, without smiling.

"I'm sorry, Kippy. It won't happen again."

"No, it won't," Kip said, dropping his arm. "Right?"

"Right," Missy said, a sinking feeling beginning in her stomach. Why did Kip always have to make her feel so terrible when she did uncool things? Why couldn't he just tell her once and then let it drop?

"Do you like this nail polish, Kippy?" she asked, trying to lighten the mood.

Kip looked at the bottle in Missy's hand and then looked at the colors still on the rack. He picked out a bottle and handed it to her. "Buy this one instead," he advised.

Missy looked at the bottle of rather dull, brownish-pink nail polish Kip had handed her. "Are you sure?

Buffy and I thought that the 'Sunrise Coral' would go better with my outfits."

He shook his head. "This one—it's not so loud. Buy it."

Missy put the "Sunrise Coral" back on the rack and walked toward the cashier with the bottle of "Burning Sands." She took out her wallet and was about to buy the nail polish when she looked again at the color. "Uhm, I don't really think I need any nail polish," she said, preparing to take it back to the counter.

Kip stepped in next to her. "She'll take this bottle," he said quickly. "Here, I'll pay for it."

It was no use arguing. Kip had decided that "Burning Sands" was the cool color to wear, and if Missy wasn't going to buy it, then he would buy it for her. A vision of Holly Block flashed through her mind. There would be no way Noel would be able to make Holly buy a color she hated. But Missy wasn't Holly Block, and Kip wasn't Noel Eliot. Missy watched the sales clerk ring up the purchase, and Kip hand over the money and take the package from her.

"Here," he said to Missy, "an extra Valentine's Day present."

"Thanks," she mumbled and put the nail polish in her purse. If her mother saw the bottle and asked where she got it, she'd have to tell her that she'd borrowed it from Buffy. There were only certain gifts Mrs. Cartwright let Missy accept from boys—and cosmetics were not among them. Lie, lie, lie, Missy thought. This is becoming a habit.

She followed Kip, Tink, and Buffy into Startay's Record Shop and went to her usual bin of current hits and rock music albums. Bored with the same old covers and the same songs, she wandered off into another aisle, looking for the Country-Western records. Missy didn't really like country music, and had never been farther west than Elgin, Illinois, but Kip liked Willie Nelson and some of the other country singers, so Missy at least knew who they were. Out of the corner of her eye she saw something that made her stop and walk back a few steps to take a second look. Mozart's Clarinet Quintet in A, the album cover read. Stephen would like that record, she thought.

Stephen, who had kissed her last night.

A shiver ran down Missy's spine, and she looked over toward Kip to see if he was watching her. No, he and Tink were pouring over the latest Styx jacket, and Buffy was buying a Rick Springfield album at the cash register. Missy looked for the bin marked "Woodwinds" and began thumbing through the records to see if any of the pieces the quintet had played were recorded. She recognized one of the pieces, but all of the others were a mystery to her. Suddenly she looked at all of the albums in the classical music bins: There were thousands of them. Woodwinds, brasses, strings, piano music, symphonies—the list seemed endless.

It was hopeless, Missy thought to herself. That was not her world, that foreign land of unknown instruments, girls who could quote Shakespeare as easily as another might recite a nursery rhyme, and boys who helped in the kitchen and didn't seem to need to take charge all the time. That was their world, and she didn't belong there. Her place was with Kip—Kip and The Group—where she knew all the rules and could play the game and come out a winner. Buffy was right. She would start devoting more time to Kip and stop any trouble before it started. She'd polish her nails with "Burning Sands" as soon as she got home, after they went to Lou's for a hamburger. Nobody at Lou's would offer her jasmine tea—only a coke or a Dr. Pepper. Stay with your own kind, Kip always told her, and as usual, Kip was right. Tomorrow at school she would make it clear to Stephen that she was Missy—not Melissa Anne—and that last night could not be repeated.

"Missy?" she heard Kip call, and looked up to see him beckoning her.

"Coming, Kippy," she answered, and hurried over to his side, snuggling up beside him, until he reminded her about the Public Display of Affection rule, at which point she stepped back, no longer quite so close to him.

Eight

"MELISSA?" STEPHEN'S voice rang above the din of
students pouring out of classrooms at the sound of the
bell.

Missy pretended not to hear him and hurried down
toward her locker. She had purposely come late to English to avoid having to talk to Stephen before class, and
now if she could get away from him, she would be relatively safe for the rest of the day.

"Melissa?" Stephen called again, close behind her.

There was nothing to do but face him, so Missy
turned around.

Stephen smiled, pleased that he had caught up with
her. He brightened even more the closer he came to
her. "I was afraid you didn't hear me," he said, a bit
out of breath. "You look terrific in that dress. Is it new?"

Missy fingered the collar of her Kelly green shirt
dress and shook her head. "No, I've had it for a while."

"You'd look great in a burlap sack," Stephen flat-
ered, as they continued down the hall and stopped

before her locker. "When you were late to English I
thought maybe you weren't coming, that you had gotten sick or something. I was awfully glad to see you
when you finally walked in," he said, taking her hand.

Missy froze. There was no way out—she would have
to tell him right now. She gently wriggled her hand
away from his grasp and began to speak. "Look, Stephen," she began slowly, the task made even more dif-
ficult by the puzzled, slightly worried look in Stephen's
eyes, "I had a wonderful time at your party Saturday
night."

"So did I," Stephen interrupted. "Holly and the others thought you were a real find."

"And I liked them, too," she said sincerely. "But
things are...well...I don't know just how to put this,"
she hesitated.

Stephen simply looked at her, waiting for her to say
what was on her mind.

"What I mean to say," she began again, "is that even
though I had a good time, I can't come to your parties
any more, and we can't meet and...hold hands or anything. It just isn't possible."

"What did I do?" Stephen asked, bewildered.

"Oh, it's not you, believe me—you're one of the nicest
boys I've ever met. It's me—it's something that was
going on long before you ever moved here. See, I'm Kip
Morgan's girl," Missy finally said, "and that means I
stick by him—always. I belong to him."

"But that's crazy!" Stephen exclaimed. "Come on,
Melissa—this isn't the Middle Ages. You don't *belong*
to anyone! Nobody does—you're an individual, free to
do and be with anyone you choose."

Missy interrupted. "Yeah, I know, but I mean...I'm

not just an individual. I'm part of Kip and The Group and I have to act the way I'm supposed to act."

"You mean the way Kip orders you to act," Stephen said coldly.

Missy's cheeks burned as though she had been slapped. "No, the way it's best for me to act. Kip has been very upset with me lately."

"Oh, and we mustn't displease His Royal Highness," Stephen said sarcastically.

"There's no use talking to you," Missy said, her voice rising with anger. Suddenly she felt a hand on her shoulder.

"Is he giving you a hard time?" Kip asked, having come up behind her.

"No, no, Kippy—we were just arguing about...*The Scarlet Letter,*" she told him, glad that Kip had saved her, once again.

"Haven't you got better things to do than argue with girls about books?" Kip asked Stephen with disdain.

"If you think I'm going to start dueling with you in the middle of a crowded hall, Morgan, you're nuts. Just say 'there's only room in this school for one of us, partner,' and we'll call it a draw," Stephen said coolly, folding his arms across his chest.

Kip just stared at him, not accustomed to having so little effect on a classmate. He put his arm around Missy's shoulder—and watched a hurt look cross Stephen's face. Having found the spot in which he could wound Stephen, Kip held Missy closer to him and kissed her on the side of her cheek. "Come on, Mistletoe," he said as Missy looked up at him, shocked by his Public Display, "The Group is waiting for us at our table."

"Yes, don't be late to the Command Performance," Stephen said loudly.

"Stick with your own kind," Kip told Stephen as he turned on his heel, his arm still around Missy.

Stephen said nothing in reply.

Although she didn't dare turn around to see for herself, Missy could feel Stephen's eyes on her as she and Kip walked the whole length of the hall, his letter-sweatered arm around her shoulders. She closed her eyes to see him more clearly, his green eyes clouded with a hurt look, his mouth a straight, unsmiling line. Goodbye, Stephen, she heard her secret voice whisper.

It was only after they passed through the double doors that led to the staircase that Kip dropped his arm from her shoulder. "Lighten up, Missy. You don't look pretty when you get that worried expression on your face. It makes those gross lines near your mouth."

Missy lightened up as she and Kip descended the stairs and entered the cafeteria, making their way through the crowd to their table where the rest of The Group was already waiting.

Nine

MISSY PULLED back the curtain and looked out her bedroom window at the dirty heaps of melting snow in the backyard. Snow and soot—an ugly combination which only added to the cold grayness of the March afternoon. She wiped her nose with the crumpled Kleenex in her hand and closed the curtains, pulling her blue quilted bathrobe more tightly around her. Maybe she should ask Mom to turn up the heat, she thought. Or maybe her fever was coming back and she had the chills.

"Knock, knock," her mother said, standing outside the bedroom door, a wicker tray in her hands. "Tea-time."

"Oh, terrific," Missy said as Mrs. Cartwright came in and set the tray on the night table. A rotund, flowered china teapot, two matching cups and saucers, a plate of buttered English muffins, and a glass jar of marmalade filled the tea tray.

"My nose must be getting unstuffed," Missy said,

sniffing the fragrant steam that escaped from the spout of the teapot. "That tea smells wonderful."

"A surprise," Mrs. Cartwright said, pulling up a chair next to the night table. "I thought that after five days in bed with the flu you could use a treat. In fact, on a day like today we could all use a little something to make us feel better. March in Chicago is not exactly one of life's little pleasures."

"No, it seems like everybody has been getting sick. Kip said that Buffy has also come down with it," Missy told her, taking the cup her mother gave her.

"Do you think that Kip will be able to bring your homework over tonight? What was it he had to do last night?"

"Meet with the Spring Carnival committee. He's in charge, as usual," she said, clearing her throat. "They were making up the booth assignments."

"Well, I still don't see why he couldn't just run the homework by on the way to his meeting. This is the second night he's called to say he couldn't bring it over," Mrs. Cartwright said, biting into a muffin.

Missy sipped the tea and inhaled the delicately scented steam. A light trace of flowers lingered on her tongue even after she had swallowed the tea. "What is this stuff, Mom? It tastes like flowers!"

Mrs. Cartwright smiled. "I knew you'd like it. Jasmine tea—they put dried jasmine petals in with the tea to perfume it. I remember my roommate in college used to brew up jasmine tea and serve it to her boyfriends. She thought it gave her an air of mystery," Mrs. Cartwright said, laughing.

Jasmine tea, Missy thought as she took another sip. So this is jasmine tea. A faraway vision of Stephen's woodwind quintet, of Holly Block and Noel, and the brown mugs of cider and jasmine tea flashed through her mind. Wouldn't you know that Stephen and Holly drank such lovely stuff. Missy sighed and reached for a muffin.

"That bad, huh?" her mother said quietly. "Want to talk about it?"

"About what?" Missy asked, surprised by her mother's question.

"About whatever made you sigh that deeply. Sighs like that should be reserved for old ladies looking at photo albums, not sixteen-year-old girls."

"It's nothing, really. I guess I'm just sick of being cooped up in this room while Kip and the others are planning the carnival and the April Showers Dance," Missy told her.

"Is that really all?" her mother asked, refilling her own cup and pouring a little hot tea into Missy's.

Missy didn't answer but chewed her muffin, licking the bittersweet orange marmalade from her fingers. "Mom?" she said, after a while.

"Hmmm?"

"How do you know if you're happy?"

"Well," Mrs. Cartwright began, "usually if you have to ask, you're not. But sometimes part of you can be happy about something and another part of you can be unhappy about something else—you know, like the day you graduated from junior high and Jimmy broke his ankle on the way home from the ceremony. Your Dad and I were happy for you, but winding up in the emergency room with Jim certainly took the sparkle out of things. Remember?"

"How could I forget?" Missy grumbled. "Half the

family waiting on the front porch for us to arrive for the lunch you made, and the four of us sitting in fancy clothes waiting in the hospital for Jimmy's X-rays to develop. What a mess."

Mrs. Cartwright shook her head. "That brother of yours was always getting himself into trouble. I think they held a special chair open for him in the emergency room he was there so often."

Missy took another sip of tea and thought for a moment. "I don't think that's exactly what I meant, though, about being happy. I mean, well, did you ever think that you were happy, that you had everything to be happy about, but that something inside just refused to be happy?"

"Yes," her mother said, nodding slowly. "Yes, I have."

"And what did you do?" Missy asked, tilting her head to one side and looking up at her mother.

"Well, I sat myself down and tried to figure out why I was supposed to be happy, and whose idea of happiness I had. Then once I got that straight I thought about what *my* idea of happiness was—and if it was the same as the other idea. If it wasn't—then I knew why I wasn't happy." She took another sip of tea and looked at her daughter. "Does that help?"

"Oh, yeah," Missy said brightening up a bit and reaching for another muffin. "It helps a lot."

Mrs. Cartwright got up from her chair and took her teacup and saucer in her hand. "I'm going to go downstairs and get dinner started. I'll leave the tea up here with you—you know what the doctor said about plenty of fluids. I thought we'd have baked chicken and rice, okay?"

"Fine," Missy said absently, as her mother walked out the bedroom door into the hall.

Mrs. Cartwright began to go down the stairs when she turned and walked back to the doorway of Missy's room. "Miss?" she said.

"Yes?" Missy answered, surprised to see her mother return.

"Try not to think too hard," Mrs. Cartwright said softly before she turned and started down the stairs to the kitchen.

Ten

"OKAY, I'M going to go to Mrs. Walker's room to get the posterboard and the magic markers. Poodie will meet me there, and then we'll come down to the student lounge and wait for you. You think you'll be done by then?" Buffy asked.

"Sure, all I have to do is pick up the mimeo sheet with next week's French assignments on it. Madame Luce didn't have time to do them before class, so she told us to pick them up at the Foreign Language teachers' office at the end of the day. I'll probably get to the student lounge before you will," Missy told her.

"Later," Buffy called over her shoulder as she dashed down the hall in the opposite direction from Missy.

Missy knocked on the door of the faculty room and Señora Lopez, the Spanish teacher, answered. "Did Madame Luce leave some mimeo sheets for her third period class?" Missy inquired.

Mrs. Lopez reached over on the shelf near the door

and handed Missy the assignment schedule, closing the door as Missy thanked her and turned to leave. Well, that didn't take long, Missy thought as she ran down the stairs and entered the student lounge on the first floor. Thirsty, she dug inside her purse for change and walked over to the soda machine, putting the money in the slot marked "Grape." If Kip were here, he'd tell her not to drink it because it turned her mouth all purple and that was definitely uncool, but Kip had tennis practice, and the purple lips would have worn off by the time she saw him. She reached in the slot where the can came tumbling down and she retrieved the soda.

"You're going to match your mimeo sheet," a girl's voice behind her said.

Missy spun around to see Holly Block, decked out in a red flowered kimono top, standing behind her. Her long black hair hung freely to her waist, and a shoulder-strapped leather school satchel was slung over one arm. "Holly!" Missy said warmly. "I haven't seen you in months. How are you?"

"Surviving," Holly answered with a big smile. "How about you?"

"Busy," Missy said, rolling her eyes.

"Yes, I saw your name in the *Highlander* in that article about the plans for Spring Carnival and the April Showers Dance. You're in charge of what?"

"I'm not really in charge of anything myself, but Kip is in charge of the whole thing and I'm his assistant."

"Oh, yeah," Holly said, nodding, "Kip Morgan."

Missy was quiet for a moment and then went ahead with the question that was on her mind. "Uhh, do you still play with the quintet?"

"Every Sunday night, for worse or for worse," Holly joked.

Missy laughed. "I still think about that evening every now and then. I had such a good time listening to all of you."

"It was fun having you. It may be the only time in history that we ever get applause."

"Is, umm, Stephen all right? I mean, we're in the same English class, but we don't talk much, uhh..." Missy tried to explain.

"Look, Stephen told me the whole story—you don't have to feel funny about mentioning it. It's just sad that things worked out that way, that's all. Too bad we can't have everything we want, all at the same time, all in one warm heap," Holly said, shrugging her shoulders. "But we can't—I guess we all have to make choices somewhere along the line." Holly glanced up at the clock on the wall. "Ooh, speaking of choice—I'm the poetry editor of *Wordsmith* this year, and I'm supposed to be choosing poems for our issue at this very moment."

"Oh, and the friends I was supposed to meet here just walked in," Missy said, waving at Buffy and Poodie who came in the room and took seats under the clock.

"Good seeing you again, Melissa. Take it easy," Holly said as she hoisted her briefcase over her shoulder and dashed out the door.

Missy opened her can of soda, threw the ring in the trash, and walked over to the couch where Buffy and Poodie were sitting. She took a sip of the grape soda, wiped her mouth and sat down next to Buffy. "Boy, am I thirsty," she said.

Poodie shifted her position on the couch. "You

wouldn't get so thirsty if you didn't dry out your mouth talking to weirdos," she said, putting a stick of gum in her mouth. "That red thing she had on was really gross."

Missy kept still for a moment before she answered. "It's Japanese—a short kimono."

"Still gross," Buffy agreed. "And all that black hair—she looks like that woman on *The Addams Family.*"

"Yeah, Morticia!" Poodie giggled. "Next thing you know Missy'll be seen talking to Uncle Fester!"

Missy shook her head. "Holly's okay. I think her hair is pretty."

"Well, if I were Kip Morgan's girl, I wouldn't risk it by talking to a weirdo," Poodie answered. "Why waste your time?"

"I wasn't wasting my time," Missy said rather angrily. "Holly's really very nice, and she plays the piano and writes poetry—it's not a waste of time at all talking to her. Besides, since when is it a crime to talk to somebody?"

"What's going on here?" Kip's voice echoed from the doorway. He walked over to the group on the couch, an annoyed expression on his face. "I could hear you guys halfway down the hall. What's all the shouting about?"

"We weren't shouting, Kippy. It's just that when Buffy and Poodie came in I was talking to this girl who was in my English class last year who plays the piano and wrotes poems and is very nice. And we said goodbye right away when they came, and I came over here and Poodie and Buffy told me that I shouldn't waste my time talking to Holly because she looks weird. And she doesn't even look weird—she just wears these Japanese tops and has real long dark hair. That's all." Missy finished her speech and looked up at Kip.

Kip looked at the three girls sitting on the couch in front of him, and then looked directly at Missy. "You should watch who you talk to, Missy," Kip said pointedly.

"What?" Missy said loudly, her eyes growing wide.

"I said that you should watch who you talk to. Poodie and Buffy are right," Kip repeated, his face cool and emotionless.

"See?" Poodie needled.

"Wait a minute," Missy interrupted, ignoring Poodie's last remark. "Why should you tell me to watch the people I talk to when you didn't even see the person we're talking about!"

"No, I didn't see this particular weirdo, but I've seen some of the others," Kip answered, shifting his weight from one foot to the other.

"Like whom?" Missy retorted.

"Like your 'shadow.'"

"Shadow?"

"That guy whose parents know your parents. I mean, putting up with his coming over to the lunch table was bad enough, but at least then anybody could see that he was the one who barged in on us, that we had nothing to do with it. I've told you before, Missy, you've got to watch it. I've got a reputation to protect and I can't afford to have you go around ruining it, talking to weirdos and attracting the wrong element. I can't have the mistakes you make reflecting badly on me."

"Do you believe this?" Missy sputtered, turning toward Buffy and Poodie. "This is the person I've been going with for over a year and a half, and he's talking about *his* reputation and the reflection I make on him. What about me, Kip? Can't you ever think about me? Maybe I want to talk to these people—maybe I see something in them that you've never even bothered to look for in anyone. He thinks he owns me!" Missy cried to Buffy and Poodie.

Buffy looked up at Kip and then back at Missy. "Well," she said slowly, "we do have an image to protect."

"Yes," Poodie agreed, "especially Kip. He's the one who really matters in your relationship. It's your duty to follow his example."

Missy just sat there, staring at the three of them, her mouth open.

"It's like that purple soda you've been drinking again, Missy," Kip interjected into the silence. "How many times have I told you that purple lips look gross."

Missy looked up at him, her eyes flashing with anger. But coolly, without emotion she stood up from her seat. "You know what's really gross, Kip?"

"Hmm?" Kip asked as Buffy and Poodie watched from the couch.

"You." Missy said calmly, gaining in strength. "You and your tiny, frail, selfish ego. You think you're the best, Kip, at the head of the line. But you don't even know where the line begins. You're so full of yourself you can't see beyond the end of your own nose. Well, you'll have to stand in line by yourself from now on— or look for some other sucker to stand with you. Or two paces behind you, as it usually is. From now on I'm finished," Missy said as she turned toward the door. She hesitated a moment and turned back toward him.

"Here—keep this for old time's sake," she added, tossing the open can of grape soda at Kip, splattering his clothes with purple stains. "Eeooh," Missy said, wrinkling up her nose. "You look gross," she told Kip before she ran out of the student lounge, never looking back.

She ran and ran down the hall, past the cafeteria, past the gym, and out the side door into the courtyard. She threw her things on the ground and sat down on the freezing cold concrete step, burying her face in her hands. A huge sob rose from her chest and burst from her mouth, releasing the tears that stung her eyes. Unaware of the cold wind that was whipping around her, Missy huddled on the step, weeping into her palms, her bookbag, purse, and coat strewn around her.

"Hey, what's this?" a familiar voice asked as the sound of one person's footsteps came closer to her. "Melissa?"

She raised her eyes to see Stephen in his running suit standing over her, having just come from the track.

"What's going on here?" he asked, bending down to look into her face.

"Go away," she told him, covering her face again with her palms.

"I will not—not until I know what's happening here. Look, you're freezing—put your coat on," he said, picking her coat up from the ground. When she made no move to take it, Stephen draped it over her shoulders, pulling it around her. "There—at least you won't get pneumonia."

"Thanks," she managed, and slipped her arms into the coat sleeves.

"Move over," Stephen said as he made room for himself to sit down next to her. "If you've decided to stay here and freeze, then I'll freeze with you until you tell me what's going on."

They sat there on the step, Stephen with his elbows on his blue running-suited knees, his hands folded under his chin; Missy hunched over, sobbing into her hands. "How time flies when you're having fun," Stephen said, when Missy showed no signs of stopping.

Stephen shrugged his shoulders and looked at Missy. "Who do you think will win the World Series this year?" he asked her.

Missy raised her head and looked at him. "What?" she said, puzzled.

"So you haven't resigned from the human race after all," he said, running his hand over her hair. "Can't you tell me what's wrong?"

"I just threw a can of grape soda all over Kip," she mumbled, putting her hands up over her face again, the tears beginning to flow once more.

Stephen just looked at her for a moment. "Run that past me again."

Missy sniffed, "I just couldn't take it one more second. Kip was being this horrible, selfish pig, and Buffy and Poodie were going along with him and I just couldn't take it anymore."

"So?" Stephen asked, his eyes growing wide.

"So I told him off and threw a can of grape soda at him. It was an open can and it splattered all over him. He looked like a purple leopard."

Stephen wanted to be sympathetic. Every muscle, nerve, and bone in his body wanted him to be sympathetic. But the thought of Kip Morgan standing in the student lounge polka-dotted with purple spots sent him into a fit of laughter.

Missy stared at him, not believing what she was seeing. "Go ahead, laugh. What do you care—you didn't just ruin your entire life. Every one of your friends didn't just desert you."

Stephen turned toward her. "Every one of your friends didn't just desert you either. You're still stuck with me," Stephen said calmly—before he dissolved into laughter once again.

Missy continued to look at him, watching his eyes crinkle up into little slits, his cheeks puff out like red apples, the laughter rolling from his lips. And suddenly, starting with a ripple that began somewhere in her stomach, rising slowly up to her chest, a giggle escaped her own throat.

"Did you just giggle?" said Stephen gasping for breath.

Missy nodded, another giggle preventing her from speaking.

"You mean," Stephen could barely ask, "you just picked up a can of soda and tossed it at him?"

"No," Missy tried to reply, the laughter muffling her words, "I...was drinking the soda before I got mad and...it just happened to be in my hand."

The two of them fell back against the steps, completely destroyed by laughter, and continued laughing until they just lay there, exhausted.

"You okay?" Stephen finally said to Missy once he had regained his composure.

"No, not really, but I'll live," she told him, drying her eyes with the back of her hand.

He sat there for a minute, his head back against the

hard step, looking up at the darkening sky. "Well, what now, Watson?"

"Beats me, Holmes," she answered, "beats me."

Stephen struggled to get up and stood in front of Missy, looking down at her. "Come on, kid, you just got over the flu. You should get home."

"How do you know I've had the flu?" she asked, taking the hand Stephen extended to her. She pulled herself to her feet, dusted off her jacket, and ran her hand through her hair, waiting for his answer.

"You didn't show up in school for a week, and when Ms. McFadden asked if anyone knew what was wrong, Helene said that she had heard in French that you had the flu."

"You know all my secrets," Missy said, blowing her nose into a Kleenex she had found in her pocket. "I must really look a mess."

"I'm an expert at messes," he said, smiling. "You couldn't look a mess if you tried."

"That's not what Kip would have said," she told Stephen. "He would have said that I looked gross."

"He's gross."

"That's what I told him after I threw the soda at him. 'Eeoo,' I said, 'you look gross.'"

Stephen looked at Missy and again they both burst into laughter.

"Oh, there's the bus," Stephen said, trying to catch his breath and run for the bus at the same time. "Waaaaiiittt" he called out as he ran, and the bus slowed down and stopped for them at the curb.

A few students looked at Missy a bit strangely as they boarded the bus. She knew that at least one girl said, "she's been crying" to her seatmate on the bus, but Missy ignored it all and walked through to the back, sitting down next to Stephen. They rode along in silence until just before they were due to get up for their stop.

"Stephen?" Missy asked.

"Hmm?"

"You think I'm going to make it through this?"

"You're going to do just fine," he assured her, patting her hand. "Come on, old girl, this is our stop," he said as the bus rounded the curve.

They got off and began the short walk from the bus to Missy's house, Stephen's arm linked through Missy's.

"Thing is," she said suddenly, "now what am I going to do?"

"What do you mean?"

"Well, I've burned all my bridges, but I don't know where to go from here. What do I do about Spring Carnival. What about The Group at lunch? I mean, I've broken up with Kip, and I'll never trust either Buffy or Poodie again, but what about some of the others like Tish or Jimbo or friends of Kip's that I've no real reason to dislike?"

"You'll see how they act toward you. Your real friends will remain your friends no matter what—and you should remain friendly toward them. The others— well, they were probably never your real friends in the first place."

"You know," Missy mused, "you're probably right. Look what happened today with Holly."

"What happened with Holly?" Stephen asked. "Holly Block?"

Missy hadn't meant to mention that the fight with Kip had been over Stephen and his friends, but she wasn't in the mood to lie to Stephen either. "No, nothing really happened with her. It's just that Buffy and Poodie saw me talking to her, and that's sort of how the whole fight began. They said that she dressed funny, and I said that she just liked Japanese clothes, that's all."

Stephen smiled, a short laugh escaping his lips. "Holly does dress sort of funny, though, doesn't she? Even she makes jokes about her kimonos."

Missy smiled. "Yeah, but it's not funny ha-ha-, she's just herself, that's all. And when I saw her today she said she knew about the episode between us—but that didn't stop her from being friendly toward me. I mean, she's one of your best friends, and there I was, being horrible to you, and she was still my friend."

"You weren't horrible to me—I just put you in an awkward situation, that's all. I hadn't realized that the line between those in The Group and those outside was tougher to cross than the border between East and West Berlin."

"Yeah, and here I am on the other side," she said to Stephen, "free." She walked along and kicked a piece of ice with the toe of her boot. "I don't know where to start. My whole life is going to change. You're wise, Stephen. Tell me what to do."

"I'd have thought you'd be sick of a boy telling you what to do," Stephen answered her, shaking his head. "I can't tell you what to do—nobody can." Stephen was quiet for a moment and then turned to look at Missy. "You could probably still patch it up, you know. He'd most likely take you back, and by tomorrow morning things would be almost back to normal."

Missy shook her head. "No, I don't want to go back.

Even if I could wave a magic wand and roll back the time to before the argument, I wouldn't want to. Once your eyes are opened you simply can't shut them again."

"Some people can."

"Well, I can't. It's just that once you've started making decisions for yourself you realize just how many there are to make. I mean, from now on it never ends."

"Yeah, but my mom says that you get to a point where you've made so many decisions you just sort of get used to doing it."

"Stephen?" she asked quietly.

"Hmmm?"

"Do you think everybody is as scared as I am?"

"Yes," he said without hesitation, "everybody is."

Missy nodded her head. "I thought so. I just don't know where to begin."

They walked through the backyard up the back steps that led to the Cartwrights' kitchen. The window over the kitchen sink was open, and she could hear her mother running water inside.

"Missy? Is that you?" Mrs. Cartwright called.

"Yes," Missy answered. She paused for a moment as Stephen turned to go. "Stephen?" she said, and he spun around to face her. "I think I'll start calling myself Melissa."

Eleven

"THAT FIRST day at school after the fight was the hardest," Melissa told Holly as she bit into her tuna fish sandwich, "expecially lunch time. I don't know what I would have done if it hadn't been for you."

"Don't be silly," Holly said, scraping a plastic spoon along the rim of her empty yogurt container. "If I didn't eat lunch this period, somebody else would have. What is this, Day Ten?"

"Yes," Missy said, taking a sip of milk through the straw in the carton, "Day Ten since I told off the great Kip Morgan."

"See, it hasn't been that bad."

"No," Missy agreed, "not too bad. Except for that meeting in the hall the other day. There they were— Kip, Buffy, Tink, and Poodie—all coming down the hall together, and there I was, coming straight at them in the opposite direction. So I just started to count, really slowly—one, two, three, four—and tried not to act nervous or upset. That counting trick really helps, you were right. And I kept counting and counting, and just as I got to the point where we were going to pass each other I looked them all straight in the eye!"

"No kidding!" Holly said, licking the yogurt lid. "I don't think I'd have had the nerve to do that."

"Well, now that the hurt has started to pass I'm furious at the way Kip treated me, and I'm just not going to cringe every time I see him in the hall. That's what he wants me to do—that will be his victory."

"So? What did they do?"

"Kip looked away—he wouldn't meet my eyes at all, but Poodie and Buffy were the best part. Poodie was walking slightly ahead of Buffy, and just before we passed each other Poodie dropped her notebook—I guess she was nervous, too. But Buffy didn't realize that Poodie was going to stop and bend down, so Buffy kept walking, and bumped into Poodie and almost fell over her. Definitely uncool, as Kip would say. Oooh, to think of all the times I let him say that to me..."

"Forget it," Holly told her, "it doesn't do you any good to waste energy on being angry about something that's over. You spent enough time and effort on all that while it was going on—don't use up any more of yourself now that it's all over."

"I *wasted* time and effort, you mean," Melissa corrected her.

"Oh, I don't know; I don't really believe in the idea that you can waste time. What you did is what you did. The important thing is not to look back, and get on with it. Like my writing, for instance. My Mom was always telling me to write something for *Wordsmith* when I was a freshman, but I never did. I mean, I had

lots of ideas for poems and stories and things, but somehow I just never sat down and wrote them out. I don't
know whether I was shy, or lazy...well, anyway, last
year I wrote this story and some poems, and they took
the poems, and this year I'm poetry editor. So now my
Mom keeps saying, 'Look at all the time you wasted,'
that I could have been on *Wordsmith* from the very
beginning. Well, I'm on it now—so what does it matter
what went on before?"

"I guess it doesn't," Melissa agreed, "but still, what
did I get from all that time I spent fooling around with
crepe paper, hanging fishnet and paper fish from the
ceiling of the gym so that it would seem as though we
were dancing 'under water'?"

Holly laughed and shook her head. "Well, I still don't
think you wasted time—at least now you know what
you don't want. Most people don't even know that!"

"Well, *I* know what I don't want—to be queen of any
more Highland Park dances," Melissa told her, crum-
pling up the wax paper her sandwich had come wrapped
in.

Holly looked intently at Melissa. "Are you sure?"
she said quietly.

"No," Melissa answered glumly, resting her chin on
her hands.

"Come on, let's get out of this place," Holly said suddenly before Melissa could become any moodier. "Come
on up to the *Wordsmith* office. Ms. McFadden brought
a hotpot—we can make a cup of jasmine tea." She got
up from the table rearranging the multicolored Indian
embroidered dress she had belted with a long magenta
sash. She noticed Melissa looking at her with an
amused grin. "All right, all right, I know I look like the

queen of the gypsies—look, you've got to grab a crown wherever you can get it. You got yours at the winter carnival—I got mine from the gypsies. Come on, let's go before somebody asks me to tell his fortune," Holly teased.

Suddenly Holly turned toward Melissa and flashed a warning look. "Start counting," she whispered as Kip and Poodie headed toward them. As Poodie spotted Melissa she grabbed Kip's hand, but as they walked by one another there were no looks of recognition that passed between any of them.

"You know what's going to happen now?" Melissa told Holly as they went up the stairs to the *Wordsmith* office.

"What?"

"Poodie's going to get a lecture on how hand-holding counts as a Public Display of Affection, and is definitely uncool," Melissa said.

"Oh, horrors!" Holly said, her hands flying to her cheeks as if shocked.

"Grievous, definitely grievous," Melissa added in mock disapproval as they entered the tiny side office of the English faculty room which served as the *Wordsmith* headquarters.

"Here, sit down," Holly said, pulling out a chair at the long conference table that took up almost all of the room. "I'll make the tea."

Just as Melissa sat down the door opened and Stephen came in accompanied by Ms. McFadden who continued on into the large, outer office.

"So!" he exclaimed, pleased to see Melissa, "the resident gypsy has finally kidnapped you and brought you here."

"I knew I should never have worn this dress," Holly muttered as she took the hotpot out of the drawer and went out to fill it from the drinking fountain in the hall.

"Everything okay?" Stephen asked Melissa.

"Fine," she answered brightly. "We just ran into His Majesty in the hall, but there was no scene."

"Good," Stephen said, sitting down at the table. "The more time that passes the less chance of a scene there will be."

"I sure hope so," Melissa answered.

"Hope what?" Holly asked as she came back with the brimming hotpot.

"Hope that there won't be any more scenes between Kip and me."

"Ancient history," Holly replied, plugging in the pot. "Jasmine tea all around?" she asked, inspecting the tea supply on the bookshelves next to the conference table.

"Mmm," Melissa said, "I'd love some. You know, my Mom said that her roommate in college used to serve all her boyfriends these little china cups of jasmine tea. She thought it gave her an air of mystery."

"Sounds like my kind of girl," Holly laughed.

"Maybe that's what I need," Melissa mused, "a little mystery." She pulled a lock of her long, shiny blond hair around in front of her face like a veil. "Do I look mysterious?" she asked Stephen in a low voice.

"I like you the way you are," he answered softly.

Melissa blushed slightly, not used to Stephen's compliments. How different he was from Kip, never judging her, taking her for exactly what she was. Still, on her own, she had begun to make some slight changes in herself. Without Kip and the group around to criticize every article of clothing she put on, every color of nail polish she wore, Melissa could now wear what she felt like wearing, not what she was expected to wear. Like this morning, for instance. She had automatically begun to put on her gray flannel pants, oxford cloth shirt, and navy monogramed cardigan when she looked at herself in the mirror. Dull, she thought to herself. I look dull. She thought about Holly and Caitlin, and the wild outfits that some of the girls on *Wordsmith* wore. She laughed out loud when she thought of herself parading around Highland Park in a bright turquoise kimono or Mexican peasant dress with multi-colored embroidery. No, she told herself—that's Holly, not you. But who are you? she asked her reflection in the mirror.

"I'm not sure," the face in the mirror replied.

It'll take time, Melissa decided. I can't find out who I am overnight. It would indeed take time.

So, Melissa had worn the gray flannel pants and navy sweater to school this morning—but she added the bright purple scarf that her mother bought her for Christmas but that Kip had forbidden her to wear. "An excellent beginning," as Stephen would say.

"Hey, earth to Melissa," Holly summoned, handing Melissa a cup of the flowery tea. "Boy, you were miles away."

Melissa laughed, taking a sip from the white Styrofoam cup. "No, not really miles away—just a couple of hours back."

The main office door suddenly opened, and Ms. McFadden walked in, a sheaf of papers in her hands. "Manuscripts, folks. I've gone through all of them and I've made a list of the things I think we should accept for the next *Wordsmith* issue. I'll just hold on to my list until all of you make up your minds. Then we can have an editorial meeting and fight for the things we each want in. Okay?"

Stephen nodded. "Are the short stories in there too?"

"Yes—including yours," she answered, smiling. "You don't have to list your own stories when you make up your 'best bets' sheets—we'll all assume that you want your own things in the issue." Ms. McFadden noticed Melissa sitting at the table, quietly drinking her tea. "Ah, so the unsinkable combination of McRae and Block have lured you into our midst, Melissa. Have you written something for us yet?"

Melissa shook her head. "Oh, no—I've never done any creative writing."

"But she has lots of ideas," Stephen said quickly. "She just needs to sit down and put them all on the paper."

"You should," Ms. McFadden told her. "Your essays in class are always very well done. I think you might turn out to be quite a good writer. That is, if you want to submit some things to us. Nobody has to write for *Wordsmith*, remember—don't let these two pressure you into writing if you don't really want to. Writing is work—and pleasure—but you shouldn't feel you have to prepare something for us just because you're friends with the people on the staff."

"But I'd like to write something," Melissa said. "I just don't know how to start."

"Follow the age-old writers' rule," Ms. McFadden said, smiling. "Write about what you know."

"Yeah, Melissa, you know—international spy rings, oil billionaires in Texas, mountain climbing expeditions to Mount Everest, just the usual thing," Holly explained.

"What are we going to do with her," Ms. McFadden said, shaking her head at Holly as she started out the door.

"Send me off to Paris with money enough to live for twenty years, and an apartment with huge windows overlooking the river Seine," Holly told them, whirling around her chair so that her skirts billowed out around her.

In the midst of her dance Noel walked in, and seeing Holly, covered his face. "Now what is she doing?" he said from beneath his hands.

"Imagining I'm in Paris, running down the Left Bank streets before I stop in a sidewalk cafe for a cup of hot chocolate and a *brioche*."

"What's a *brioche?*" Melissa whispered to Stephen.

"A roll," Stephen whispered back, winking.

"Not just any roll," Holly countered. "Have you no respect for French bakers? *Brioche* are those little eggy buns that have a topknot and are so buttery you can just…"

"She'll never get over that trip she took last summer," Noel muttered, pulling Holly out the door. "Come on, we've got orchestra rehearsal and there's the bell."

"Wait! My books," Holly cried, dashing back into the office. She looked over at Stephen as she headed out the door. "Tell Melissa about the plans for Saturday night, okay?"

"Come *on!*" Noel called from the hall.

"Boys!" Holly grumbled to Melissa, smiling, as she scooped up her belongings and tore out the door.

Melissa looked at Stephen and shook her head slowly. "Holly's really something."

"You're really something," Stephen said softly, his green eyes warm and admiring.

"You too," she smiled. Then suddenly feeling a bit awkward saying these things in the middle of the English office, she quickly added, "What were you supposed to tell me about Saturday night?"

"Oh, that. Well, Noel has his father's car this weekend, and we're going to troop into Chicago for a movie at the 'Biograph'. They've got a Marx Brothers festival this weekend. We'll get there in time for *A Night at the Opera* and *Animal Crackers*. How does that sound to you?"

"And dinner at the Indian place where the waitresses wear those outfits?"

"*Saris,* yeah, and dinner there, too. Can you come?" Stephen asked hopefully.

"Can I! Sounds terrific!" Melissa said excitedly. "I haven't gone into Chicago since before Christmas."

"We always leave a little extra time coming in so that we can take the scenic route and drive down Michigan Avenue and over to the Outer Drive to get a look at Lake Michigan."

"I can't wait," Melissa enthused as they gathered their books. "I just can't wait."

Twelve

"AND THEN," Missy said excitedly, "we're going to this movie theater where they show all these old films, you know, with Humphrey Bogart and Greta Garbo.... Tonight will be two Marx Brothers movies," Melissa told her mother as Mrs. Cartwright sat on her daughter's bed, watching Melissa get dressed.

"Well, I can say one thing for that new crowd of yours—they certainly seem less restrictive about the clothes they wear. You're finally making use of half the things in your closet that you've gotten for birthday and Christmas gifts. I could never understand what was wrong with all of those clothes, but you were so insistent that they were 'definitely uncool' that it wasn't worth arguing with you. I see you've dug out that lovely blouse Aunt Elaine gave you last year."

Melissa looked at herself in the mirror. Now what in the world had Kip found to criticize in this silky, robin's-egg blue top with its stand-up Mandarin collar and long, full sleeves? She tied the narrow gold rope belt more tightly around the high waist of her front-pleated white wool pants, and smoothed her hand over the long braid of her hair that she had caught at the top with a wrapping of thin, gold cord. A brushful of light, rosy blush and some clear lip-gloss completed the picture. "How do I look?" she asked her mother.

"Gorgeous," Mrs. Cartwright answered. "It's good to see you in some bright colors rather than that constant navy blue. Maybe now you can get some wear out of that purse I bought for you on sale that wasn't returnable."

"Great!" Melissa said, remembering the gold mesh pouch that she had loved but that Buffy and Kip had absolutely vetoed. She dug into her bottom drawer and found the purse, still wrapped in its original tissue paper. "Oh, Mom," she cried, running over to the bed and giving her mother a hug, "it's just perfect!"

The doorbell sounded and Mr. Cartwright called from downstairs. "Missy—I mean, Melissa—Stephen's here."

"I look okay?" Melissa asked her mother again.

"Oh, for goodness' sakes..." her mother began.

"You're right, I know I look fine," Melissa answered, turning around for one last glimpse in the mirror.

"That's better—compliment yourself for a change," Mrs. Cartwright said as they went out of the bedroom and Melissa dashed ahead, down the stairs to a waiting Stephen.

"I don't believe you," Stephen exclaimed when he saw her, "you look sensational!" He just stood there watching her, not moving and not saying anything.

"You look great, too," she answered, a bit embarrassed. He does, she thought to herself, in his dark blue corduroy pants, thick fisherman's sweater, and dark green parka.

"Well, I sure don't look as dressed up as you do," he began to apologize.

"You both look terrific," Mrs. Cartwright said as a horn honked outside. "Hurry up, Melissa, the others are waiting for you," she said as Melissa put on her coat and wrapped her scarf around her neck. "Now have a great time and drive carefully," she added.

"Oh, don't worry about Noel, Mrs. Cartwright," Stephen assured her. "He's a really careful driver. Besides, how fast can you go in a station wagon?" he asked smiling.

"Just be careful," Mr. Cartwright told them as they walked out the door and Melissa waved to the crowd in the car.

"We will," they chorused as they ran down the walk and climbed into the back seat.

"What were you doing in there," Caitlin asked them as they squeezed together and shut the car door, "discussing current trends in the stock market? I thought you were never going to come out, and it was getting hot in here."

"It wasn't that long," Stephen told her, giving Melissa a wink. "It just took me a while to regain consciousness after I got a look at Melissa."

"Yeah, I really like your hair that way," Holly said, turning around in the front seat to face them. "You look like one of those ads for how your hair can look if you use the right shampoo—you know, 'no frizzies.' How'd you get it so smooth? Whenever I pull my hair straight back and braid it there are still all these little wisps that stick out."

"I like all those wisps," Noel said, watching the road, his hands on the steering wheel.

"I guess it just depends on the kind of hair you have," Melissa said, "but you're the last one who has to worry about that. Anyway, I just used some of that conditioner stuff that comes in a tube."

"Gee, this is fascinating," Dylan said to Stephen. "Tell me, what kind of soap did you use in the shower this morning?"

"All right, all right, we get the hint," Holly told him. "But I don't see anything wrong with girls exchanging beauty secrets. We can't always discuss the burning questions of literature and great art, you know. Sometimes lip gloss and perfume can be just as interesting as e.e. cummings," Holly said.

Noel flashed her a look of amusement and shook his head, laughing.

"Well, almost as interesting," Holly muttered as the car rolled down the road toward the bright city lights.

"We'll go past the turnoff we're supposed to take to get to the restaurant, ride down near the lake, and then take a short trip up Michigan Avenue past the John Hancock building and Water Tower Place where all the fancy shops are. Then we'll head back north toward Old Town," Noel advised as they rode along onto the Outer Drive that bordered Lake Michigan and connected the far north side of Chicago with the center of the city.

The March lake was no longer ice-capped, but angry waves lashed up on the shore, and the dark beach had a menacing look under the moonlit sky. Melissa shivered slightly and huddled closer to Stephen in the car

He looked down at her and smiled. "It's a little scary, all that foaming water in the white moonlight, huh?" Stephen whispered, putting his arm around her shoulder.

Melissa looked up at him amazed. "But I didn't even say anything—how could you know what I was thinking?"

"Because I was feeling the same way."

"Look, the Water Tower's all lit up," Dylan announced as they drove past the old relic of the Chicago Fire that stood like a white castle in the middle of the modern, bustling city. They continued driving down the broad boulevard and peered out the windows of the car at the fashionable shops, well-dressed people, and sparkling city lights that bordered the street on both sides. After a few blocks, Noel turned down a side street and drove until Melissa saw a sign that read "Shanti."

"Here we are," Holly cried as the car slowed down and Noel began pulling into a parking spot near the restaurant.

"'Shanti'?" Melissa asked Stephen.

"It means 'peace' in Hindi, the Indian language the owners of the restaurant speak," Stephen explained.

So much to learn, Melissa thought to herself as she got out of the car. Her heart raced with excitement as the group entered the restaurant.

"Oh, it's like a scene out of the Arabian Nights," Melissa exclaimed as their eyes adjusted to the dim light. The walls were hung with brightly colored Indian tapestries and huge brass plates, and little candles in colored glass holders flickered throughout the restaurant like stars. The hostess, dressed in a long, flowing chiffon *sari* that wrapped and folded itself around her like a huge, body-length scarf, showed them to a white-clothed table under a painting of brown-skinned, long-haired dancing girls with eyes as dark as black grapes.

Melissa looked at the menu Stephen handed her, and didn't recognize a single familiar dish. A feeling of panic rose in her throat, and for a moment Melissa was afraid she might start to cry. You don't fit in here, the little voice within her began to say.

"Shall I order for you?" Stephen asked her. "The first time I ate in an Indian restaurant I didn't recognize one thing on the menu. I won't get anything too spicy, I promise."

Melissa looked at Stephen's warm, friendly face, and wondered what on earth she had been getting all uptight about. She did fit in here—these people were her friends.

Stephen and the others gave the waitress their orders, and soon she returned with platters of wonderful smelling curries, each a different color—red, green, yellow, and dark brown. In tiny bowls were hot and sweet relishes called chutneys made out of all sorts of exotic ingredients like mangoes and dates. Melissa took a little of everything including some rice and a white sauce from a big bowl in the center of the table.

Hesitantly she took some of the white sauce on her fork and tasted it slowly. Yogurt! She had found something recognizable after all! Filled with daring, she sampled each of the things on her plate. Only the red curry was not to her liking—the fiery hot chili peppers brought tears to her eyes.

"Eat a little of the yogurt to cool off your mouth," Holly whispered when she saw Melissa's problem.

Melissa followed her advice—and took a long drink

of water—the rest of the meal passed without a repeat chili disaster. After big cups of spiced tea and sweets tasting of roses from their rosewater syrup, they decided to try and move—and walk up to the nearby theater.

"Oh, I ate too much," Holly groaned as she pushed her chair away from the table and rose to put on her coat.

"No Milk Duds for you at the movie," Noel taunted.

"Yech, don't even mention anything else to eat until tomorrow," said Caitlin.

"Ready to go?" Stephen asked Melissa, who was still seated, taking a last look around the restaurant.

"Just looking around so that I can remember everything," she told him happily. How different Stephen's "Ready to go?" was from Kip's usual "C'mon." It was nice to be asked whether you were ready to leave—not just ordered to move.

They paid the check—Stephen insisting to Melissa that it was his treat—and went outside, down the street to the movie house.

The night air was chilly, but after the spicy food everyone was energized, and the cold wind made them even more alert and bouncy.

Holly began to sing a chorus of "Maxwell's Silver Hammer," the old Beatles' song as she walked along holding Noel's hand. Soon Noel had joined her, then Dylan and Caitlin joined in. Melissa marveled at the ease she felt, walking down the busy Chicago street, her friends singing songs around her, nobody caring how cool or uncool anyone looked, just having a good time. By the time they reached the theater the food had settled, and everyone was ready to sit down and feast on the Marx Brothers.

The theater was crowded with all types of people—kids from the suburbs who like Melissa and her friends had driven in to Chicago; city kids whose elegant shabbiness marked them as students at some of the city's fancier private schools; college students taking a break from term papers; and adults, even old people, some of whom could probably remember when these Marx Brothers movies first came out.

It's a huge world out here, Melissa thought to herself—so much bigger than she'd ever suspected sitting in front of the video machine in Buffy Sanders's den—and I'm becoming a part of it.

After the movies, which were even better and more hilarious than Melissa had ever remembered them to be, they walked slowly back to the car, savoring the good feelings the movies had given them.

It was a long drive back to Highland Park, and even Holly was quiet, which, as Noel remarked, was a landmark occasion. Melissa yawned and curled herself up against Stephen's shoulder, dozing contentedly as Noel guided the car back home. They had planned on stopping at one of the coffee houses near the theater so that Melissa could taste *cappucino*—the Italian coffee drink of steamed milk, coffee, and cinnamon served in enormous mugs—but everyone was just too tired.

"Next time," Holly promised when they all agreed that they had had enough adventure for one evening.

"Next time," Melissa mumbled to herself as she snoozed, her head nestled against Stephen, his arm around her shoulder.

"What?" he asked, half asleep himself.

But Melissa had already lapsed into sleep again, and she didn't wake up until they reached Highland Park when Noel woke Stephen, who then woke Melissa to tell her that the car was in front of her house.

Thirteen

STEPHEN CAME over to the lunch table where Melissa was sitting, her cheese sandwich half-eaten in front of her.

"Hi," she said when she saw him approaching, "what took you so long?"

Stephen sat down across from her, a peculiar look on his face. "I was up in the *Wordsmith* office, looking over short story manuscripts," he said, taking his sandwich out of a brown bag.

"That's nice," Melissa told him, suddenly absorbed in a speck of dirt on the table.

"Melissa?"

"Yes?" she answered without looking up.

"Is this yours?" Stephen asked her, holding up the short story she had neatly typed and submitted without putting her name on the title page.

"Mine?"

"I knew it!" Stephen said excitedly, "I knew that you had written it. Why didn't you say something, silly?"

"What did you think of it?"

"Think of it? It was unanimous—we accepted it immediately!" Stephen told her proudly. "Everybody thought it was terrific."

"You did?" Melissa said, her eyes growing wide. "I mean, even before you knew it was mine?"

"How could I be sure it was yours if you turned it in anonymously?"

"Well, what gave me away?" she questioned, pleased with the news of her acceptance.

"Oh, the subject matter, I guess. When I first saw the title, 'The Girl Who Changed Her Name,' I thought of you, never guessing that you were the author. Then I started reading it, and I kept thinking, 'Gee, this character stops using her nickname and starts calling herself by her whole first name—that's just like Melissa.' And then suddenly it dawned on me—this *is* Melissa! But I had almost finished the story by then, so believe me, knowing that you wrote it didn't change my opinion. I liked the story from the very first page— and so did everybody else."

"Does everybody know that I wrote it?"

"No, nobody else figured it out. Most of them thought that Elizabeth Monroe wrote it."

"Hi," Holly told them. "Sorry I'm late but Ms. McFadden wanted me to write down all the acceptances for the short story manuscripts on one list." She turned toward Stephen. "Have you seen Elizabeth anywhere? I tried to find her in the yearbook office, but she wasn't there."

"No," Stephen answered, "but I don't think we need to find her."

"Oh?" Holly said. "How come?"

"Because Melissa wrote the story," Stephen boasted, enjoying being the one to break the news.

"You!" Holly cried. "Why didn't you say something?"

"Oh, because I wanted you to judge the story itself—not as my story," she told them. "I know that you always judge things anonymously at first, but I thought that somehow someone might find out—so I decided just to slip it in the submissions box with no name at all. I figured that somebody would start talking about it eventually, especially if you liked it, and that I'd tell you then."

"Well, welcome to *Wordsmith*," Holly told her as she got up from the table, preparing to leave.

"Where are you going, Holly?" Melissa asked.

"I've got to go and get that note I left for Elizabeth telling her how much I liked her writing and that she had just been made a member of the *Wordsmith* guild. Do me a favor from now on, huh—save the 'who-done-it' stuff for any mystery stories you write."

Melissa laughed. "Sorry," she told Holly, who was already off to the yearbook office. Melissa finished her sandwich and put the wrapping in the brown bag, looking over at her copy of the school newspaper that she had received in home room that morning but hadn't read yet. There on the front page was the announcement she had been dreading. "The April Showers Dance," the caption over the article read, "Who Will Be King and Queen?" She read down the alphabetical list of names until she reached "Kip Morgan," almost afraid to see whom he had chosen as his partner. "Poodie (Patricia) Hawkins," the name read. Melissa couldn't believe her eyes. So that was it all along, she thought to herself. That's why Poodie had tried to cause trouble between me and Kip, mentioning my shoes at the Valentine's Dance, always taking his side. She was never my friend at all, Melissa told herself—she was after Kip all along.

"Oh, well," Melissa said, casting the paper aside, "that was another life."

"What?" Stephen asked, looking up from his own copy of the paper.

"Nothing, nothing at all."

"Uhm, Melissa," Stephen began, putting down his paper, "I don't know whether you'll go for this idea, but... would you like to go to the April Showers Dance with me? Holly and Noel are going, and I thought that, unless you'd rather just avoid the whole thing, we might all go together. If it would be too upsetting, you know..."

"I'd love to go," Melissa told him honestly, "and I'd love to go with you."

Stephen just looked at her, not believing that it had all been so easy, that he didn't have to coax her into going. "Uhh, good, then..." he said, a bit flustered, "I guess now you girls run around and try to find dresses and then you tell us what colors they are so that we can get the right flowers, huh?"

Melissa looked at Stephen for a moment, trying to figure out what was the matter. Then all at once it struck her. "You've never been to a dance, have you?" she asked gently.

Stephen looked down at the table and shook his head. "No. My other girlfriend, Lucy, didn't believe in things like dances and that kind of stuff, so we never went."

Melissa smiled. "Don't worry—everything will turn out just fine. Only if you eat too many chili peppers, take a spoonful of yogurt to cool the fire."

Stephen looked confused. "What chili peppers? What are you talking about?"

"Nothing—it's just that I'm learning that everytime you do something you've done before, someone else in the room may be doing it for the first time. I guess if you just remember that, then you never have to worry about doing new things—chances are someone else is also trying something new. What's new to you is old to someone else—but what's old to you may be somebody else's idea of a scary adventure."

"You're really something, you know that? How'd you get so wise?"

"Hanging around with wise guys," Melissa laughed as they got up to leave the cafeteria. "I suppose I'd better go tell Ms. McFadden that I'm the one who wrote the story," she said as they started up the stairs together.

"You're just one surprise after another, Ms. Cartwright."

"That's me," Melissa agreed as they rounded the corner to the *Wordsmith* office. "That's me," she repeated, smiling to herself.

Fourteen

"DO YOU think I look dumb in this thing?" Holly asked Melissa as they stood before the mirror in the girls' washroom, combing their hair and adding more lip gloss while the orchestra took a break between dances.

"Well, it's not the usual thing people wear to an April Showers Dance, but you look very striking," she told Holly, unable to keep a straight face.

"But do I look dumb?" Holly insisted.

"No ... you look like an Indian," Melissa told her as she watched Holly rewrap the rainbow-colored chiffon sari that she had worn to the dance. With her hair pulled back into a long braid and her big dangly silver hoop earrings, Holly did indeed resemble the waitresses Melissa had seen at Shanti.

Holly looked at their reflections in the mirror. "I should have worn another dress," she decided as she started to rebraid her hair. "It's too hard to dance in this."

Melissa let Holly ramble on while they both freshened up. Funny, she thought, to find myself here at the April Showers Dance after all. Once she had accepted Stephen's invitation, Melissa found that she started worrying about going to the dance. It wasn't the idea of going with Stephen that bothered her—that part was super. It was the thought of being at the dance, seeing all of the people who had voted for her and Kip, who would now be voting for Kip and Poodie. Was it jealousy? she wondered. No, not exactly—it was more like the feeling she'd had when she and her parents drove by their old house after they'd already moved into their new one. Melissa loved the new house and her room there was twice the size of her old room. But when they turned the corner and she saw two children's faces peering out of the window of her old room, she was upset. Although she certainly did not want to be still living in that old room, she didn't want anybody else living in it either. Oh, well, she thought, putting her hair-brush away, at least she had had the nerve to come to the dance—and had worn a dress she could dance in.

She adjusted the skirt of the silky "Melissa-blue" scoop-necked dress that was embroidered all over with little flowers and had a border of white eyelet edging around the hem, the collar, and the full, puffed sleeves. The wide blue sash around her waist tied in a great big bow in the back, and her mother had lent her a blue and white Wedgewood cameo necklace that matched the color perfectly. Both she and Holly had decided to wear glittery, sheer white stockings, and Melissa had worn the same silver shoes that had caused such a fuss at the Valentine's Dance.

Having seen a picture in a magazine of a girl with a braid that started high on the top of her head and was decorated with little sprigs of silk flowers all down the length of the braid, Melissa bought some blue and white flowers and copied the style exactly. When she came down the stairs to find Stephen waiting in his dark blue suit, a camelia corsage for her in his hands, she knew that at last she was off to a dance where her clothes would not meet with criticism from her escort. "You look gorgeous," he had told her, and she saw from the look in his eyes that he meant what he said. "Maybe I should warn you," he told her with a smile as they headed out to Noel's car. "Holly is wearing a sari." Melissa told him that she already knew, that Holly had been planning her outfit for weeks. Noel seemed to think the whole thing was pretty funny, and had shown up in what he referred to as his "Colonel Sanders" white suit.

"They're made for each other," she said to Stephen as Noel and Holly walked into the dance. "How about us?" he asked her, but by then they, too, had entered the dance, and the music was too loud to be heard over.

It had been hard walking into that crowded dance, knowing that so many people knew about the break-up between her and Kip, and Melissa's heart was racing, her mouth dry. "How shall I act?" she had asked Stephen the night before the dance. "What if I see people from my old crowd? Do I say hello? What should I do?"

"What do you do in school?" he had said.

"If someone says hello, I say hello back—or if somebody looks as though he or she wants to say hello but doesn't quite have the courage, then I say hello first."

"Then there's your answer," Stephen told her. "Just

follow the same rules at the dance that you follow in school and everything will be just fine. And stop worrying so much about what everybody is thinking!" he insisted. "Most of the people will be so concerned about having their own good time and not making their own terrible mistakes that they won't have time to be gossiping about you."

"Maybe," Melissa had answered, knowing that what Stephen said was probably correct, but remaining slightly unconvinced.

But once they got inside the gym everything Stephen had said started to make perfect sense. She looked around at the wonderful decorations, the strips of clear, colored cellophane in pink, yellow, blue, and green that had been hung from the ceiling to make it look as though it were raining. Parasols in pastel colors were hanging everywhere, and at one end of the gym a huge rainbow covered half the wall. Bunches of daisies, daffodils, narcissus, and tulips were placed around the room, and pastel candles decorated the punch table.

She and Stephen danced the first two dances and were on their way to sample some of the pink lemonade punch when she saw Poodie Hawkins about to cross her path. She swallowed hard and followed Stephen's advice, prepared to say hello if Poodie greeted her, prepared to take it in stride if Poodie ignored her. But Poodie had obviously not been given any advice at all, for once she noticed Melissa, she turned and fled in the other direction.

"See—nothing to it," Stephen told her after this first crisis passed. "Now just relax and have a good time. I'm having a great time—and if anybody should be nervous, I am. Don't forget, this is my first dance."

Melissa smiled and squeezed Stephen's hand. "Thanks," she told him as they walked back onto the dance floor. Just as they were about to begin dancing she noticed Tish Honeywell and Jimbo Ryan dancing next to them.

Tish looked at her a bit timidly, but when Melissa began to smile, Tish smiled too. "How are you, Missy?" she called over Jimbo's shoulder. "You look fantastic."

"Thanks, Tish—you too," Melissa called back, and winked at Stephen, who had witnessed the whole exchange.

From that moment on Melissa began to enjoy herself—in fact enjoy herself more than she had ever done at any dance she went to with Kip. It was wonderful to be at a dance with a partner who really liked her, who wasn't watching out to see that she was acting "uncool." And there was a freedom that Melissa found at this dance—one which "Missy" had never had: the freedom to be herself. With no eyes constantly upon her, no contest results to worry about, and without the nagging pressure of being "perfect" weighing her down, Melissa felt a light, dizzying exuberance that she had never felt before. There was only one more hurdle that she would have to pass before she could truly say that the dance had been a success.

Stephen noticed the clearing of the platform where the king and queen would be crowned before Melissa did. "Melissa?" he asked her suddenly. "Would you like to go outside for a little air? It's getting kind of hot in here. I think we both could use a walk around the lake."

Melissa looked at him, wondering why he was suddenly so interested in fresh air. Then she looked over toward the little stage that had been set up with a daffodil-decorated throne—and in an instant she understood everything.

"You're the absolute best," she told Stephen, "come on—let's get our coats."

They walked over to the cloak room, hand in hand, got their wraps, and went out the side door that led to the path down to the lake. The cold air rushed around them, reminding them that April in Chicago can still feel a bit more like winter than spring. The walk down to the lake was well lit by the old street lamps that had been lighting that path for almost a century. All evening the narrow pathway had been crowded with people coming and going to the dance, but for the crowning of the king and queen all the others had gone inside.

"You okay?" Stephen asked her quietly as they came to the barrier wall that overhung the lake below.

"I'm fine, Stephen—just fine," she answered, looking out at the waves silvered by the moonlight. The sky was overcast with clouds, and the full moon was continually veiled and unveiled again as the smoky gray clouds passed before it and then moved on, rushed forward by the wind.

"I'm glad we're here, Melissa," Stephen said, moving closer to her and putting his arm around her shoulders.

"Me too," she said softly. "I'm glad you thought to come out here."

"No, no, I didn't mean that—I meant I'm glad we came to the dance together tonight," Stephen told her, the wind blowing his thick dark hair over his forehead, his bright eyes catching the light of the moon.

"I'm always glad to be with you," Melissa answered, "here, or in the *Wordsmith* office or at a Marx Brothers movie—anywhere." She looked up into his face, her cheek resting on his chest. "Thanks for everything, Stephen."

"I didn't do anything."

"Yes, yes, you did," she insisted, nuzzling against his jacket. "I don't know what I would have done without you."

"You would have done just fine," Stephen told her. "All I did was watch you become yourself—you did all the work. You changed your name, and began wearing other kinds of clothes; you made an effort to learn new things—you even wrote your short story."

"And," she said, giggling, "I threw a can of grape soda at Kip—I did that all by myself."

"Yes, you did," Stephen replied, beginning to laugh all over again. "Maybe that was your greatest stroke of genius."

"Still," she told him, "having you here made it all a lot easier."

"Well, that's what friends are for, you know—making the bad times bearable and making the good times wonderful."

"Stephen?" she asked quietly.

"Mmm?"

"You're the best friend I've ever had."

Stephen didn't answer, but instead put his other arm around her, shielding Melissa from the chilly wind.

"I used to think that I had lots of friends," she continued in a low voice. "In fact, I thought that almost everybody was my friend. But then, that night at your house when you first invited me to hear your woodwind group and meet your friends, that was the first night I wondered whether I had gotten the whole friendship

idea straight at all. After watching you and Holly and
Noel and Caitlin, seeing how warm and easy you all
were with each other, it made what I had with Kip and
The Group seem, oh, I don't know—unreal. And then
when all that happened at once with Buffy and Poodie
and then Kip..."

"Shhh," Stephen whispered, "don't think about it
now. That's all ancient history." He hugged her a little
closer, and Melissa hugged him back, her arms wrapped
tightly around his broad, warm back.

"I'll bet Kip and Poodie have been crowned by now,"
she said softly. She was quiet for a moment, obviously
upset by a new, troubling thought. "Stephen, do you
think that Kip will gloat over being crowned? I mean,
do you think he'll cause me any trouble or try to make
me feel bad about it?"

Stephen shook his head. "No—I don't think he'd do
anything like that. Who knows? Maybe he won't have
anything to gloat about this time."

"Fat chance," Melissa sighed, "he won everything
there was to win." She hugged Stephen even tighter.
"Ancient history," she repeated, "ancient history."

"It's getting pretty cold," Stpehen said as the wind
blew around them, Melissa's blond hair tickling his
face as the wind caught the short wisps that escaped
the barrette and sent them swirling against Stephen's
chin.

"Yes," she answered, looking up into his eyes. The
full moon overhead washed their faces in a cool, pearly
bath of light—but the light that shone in Stephen's
eyes was even brighter still, and warmed her like a
nighttime sun. "Will you always be my friend Stephen,
always?"

"Always," he answered, the sun-warmth spreading to the smile on his lips.

And then that warmth tingled on her lips too—when Stephen lifted her chin with his hand and gently kissed her. Unlike the hasty, shy kiss that left her bewildered and embarrassed the night he walked her home from that first party, this kiss was a summer-warm bond that forever sealed a friendship. Melissa closed her eyes and let the midnight sunbeams melt away the final traces of hurt and confusion deep within her.

Stephen stepped back, his arms still linked behind her. "We don't want to miss the last dance," he said softly.

"No," she answered, "we'd better go back."

He leaned forward and kissed her once again, and then slowly, they walked back up the path to the dance, back to the bright lights and voices, back to a world Melissa no longer feared.

"I don't see the king and queen," Melissa whispered as they dropped off their coats and reentered the gym.

"I see the queen," Stephen answered, with a smile, "she's right here, dancing with me." Melissa squeezed his hand and walked with him out onto the dance floor.

"There you are," Holly called out as she and Noel danced past them. "I guess Mr. Kip Morgan won't be so sure of himself from now on," Holly added as she whirled on by.

Melissa started to ask her what she meant, but another couple got in the way and Holly and Noel disappeared into the crowd as the lights began to dim as a signal that the next dance would be the last.

She decided to put the remark out of her mind when suddenly Stephen stopped dancing in the middle of the floor and pointed toward the king and queen's platform. "Look, Melissa—the king and queen are on the stand with their court."

Melissa looked in the direction of Stephen's hand. There with crowns and purple robes were a boy from Melissa's history class and the red-haired girl who was his date. And farther down the platform, along with the other couples who had not been chosen, were a glum Poodie Hawkins and an even more glum Kip Morgan.

"You see, Melissa," Stephen told her happily, "it was never Kip at all—it was always you. Without you Kip's nothing—you're the real winner. You had it all backwards—he won because of you."

Melissa looked again at the platform. She couldn't believe her eyes. But instead of laughing with delight she simply looked at Stephen and shook her head. "Poor Kip," she said as she moved toward Stephen and began to dance with him again. "Winning was all Kip ever had, the only thing that made him special."

Stephen hugged her close and whispered in her ear. "You're the one who's special...always special."

Melissa rested her head on Stephen's shoulder as the slow dance music sang in her ears and the lights from the candles cast huge shadows on the darkened dance floor. "What *we* have is special," she answered him, "you and I."

Stephen nodded in reply, his chin brushing against her cheek.

Melissa wanted to fix this moment in her mind forever. A dreamy smile lit her lips, and a light, breezy feeling fluttered in her chest. She nuzzled closer into Stephen's arms, her eyes still closed.

Only now did she understand what her mother meant about happiness.

When you're really happy, you don't even have to ask the question.

You already know the answer by heart.

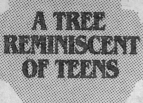

A TREE REMINISCENT OF TEENS

—Growing, Changing and Striving...

JUNIPER

28   TAF-11